THE UPTURNING
by
Sheema Biswas

Paperback 979-8-9880512-1-3

E-book 979-8-9880512-0-6

Library of Congress Control Number: 2023905971

First Paperback edition: April 2023

Written/Edited/Cover Art by Sheema Biswas

Printer Name: Draft2Digital

Publisher: Salten Publishing

To my parents

Chapter 1

When Silk Road caravans came west, the traders entertained courts with tall stories. Supernatural beasts guarded certain spice trees in the jungles of India, the traders said. Trees with gifts more precious than gold. And that many in the caravan had been torn from limb to limb by the fierce monsters, never to return. The tales entranced audiences.

Cinnamon and black pepper were common in food and medicine by then. The western world craved things more exotic. For stone flower, mace, inknuts and carom seeds - the curiosities the traders said were found in the wilds of India.

Restless seafarers inspired by the strange myths, and eager for adventure, conceived a plan for a direct sea route to the Indian subcontinent. And in 1497 the explorer Vasco da Gama sailed from Portugal to a destination point in India.

His fleet circled the Cape of Good Hope, went up the African continent, and crossed the Arabian Sea to Asia. The ships landed in Calicut, a trade hub on India's west coast the following year. Their arrival started a chain of brutal spice wars between the two countries.

The Portuguese revisited over the seasons, gaining ground with the *Zamorin* - the ruler of Calicut - with each visit. By 1503 they had control of the region. The coastal territory of Goi and the smaller islands further north became their strongholds. And these parts would remain under Portugal's rule for the next four hundred and fifty years.

Fins Island was one of those lesser islands in the Indian Ocean. The island lay about twenty-eight nautical miles west of the mainland state of Goi.

At first, the settlers who came traveled from Goi to the island every summer and vacationed here for the rest of the season. Refreshing breezes blew in from the cays and coves all year. And it was a welcome change from the soupy inland summers. In time, they built sprawling homes with garden courtyards on the shoreline and settled on the island for good.

The last of the Portuguese settlers quit Fins Island in 1943, leaving behind a legacy of churches, lighthouses and estates which stand even today. Locals who now owned the colonial villas along the shore repainted them in playful colors. As tourism picked up, some of those homes were renovated and rented out. Others were transformed into luxury resorts and hotels. And private buyers snapped up what was left.

People said the island's name likely came from '*phanas*,' the local word for jackfruit. It was a divisive fruit. And the cause of a longstanding feud between Goyans and Finsians who clashed over its very existence.

The tree grew like mad on the island's coast but not much in Goi. And the yearly name-calling began in late July when the jackfruit matured, broke from the stems and slipped into the sea. Easterly currents swept them from the islands and onto Goyan sands. The mess of rotting fruit closed down several beaches in the summer, and provoked sun loving Goyans no end.

"Backwater cretins," ticked off Goyans called Finsians. "With no civic sense."

"Control freaks," Finsians hollered back at Goyans. "With heads up a sunless place."

And so, it went. Back and forth. Like oil and water, as the saying goes. And so it was to this day.

Chapter 2

F *ins Island*
Rish watched the road from the shaded front porch of the villa. A month-long yoga retreat opened that day at Margosa, the resort he ran. And he was nervous they had overlooked something.

"How are the arrangements?" he asked P. Jha, again.

His question fell on deaf ears, again. The office manager had wandered off to glare at a chirpy group of employees waiting at the entrance for the guests.

"Ssshhhh!" Jha said, glaring at them.

But the women carried on amongst themselves and ignored the admonition. Their breathy laughter bent the flames of lighted clay lamps set on silver *thalis*, the decorative platters they held in front of them. Next to the lamps were small pots of vermilion. They would smear a smidgen of red on the forehead of arriving guests, in a welcome ritual that was the traditional greeting in the land.

"Some persons. Noisy buzzy bees," Jha said, walking up to him.

Jha drew out his tobacco pouch from his jacket and extracted a pinch of the brown stuff. He stowed the knob of tobacco under his tongue.

"I said..." Rish said.

"Forgive myself, I am hearing yourself. *Ekdum* tip top. Everything is ship-shape," Jha said to him, chewing the tobacco with a careless gusto. He slid his chin forward to hold the chewed contents in place.

His expression said he knew your intimate secrets. Those harmless indiscretions you thought interested nobody. He had them. And he made sure you knew he had them.

Rish pointed at the pouch he tried to spirit away. "Why do you do it?" he asked. He wondered why he put up with Jha. His work ethics were a disgrace.

"I am not understanding your meaning," Jha replied, crinkling his eyes.

He brushed the question aside with a snide laugh and pretended he never heard it. His smugness irritated Rish all the more.

"You know what I mean. Look around you. The disgusting stuff you spit out of your mouth is at every corner. We run a resort and spa here, for heaven's sake."

Jha pushed at the lump and flattened it, so his face looked normal. The criticism rolled over him. It meant nothing, and it went into one ear and out the other. His family's incessant nagging had not broken his addiction either. But Jha was losing his corgi's affection because of his use, and that hurt him more than anything. These days Purl waddled out of the room with an indignant glance at him when he reached for her. What could he do? He found tobacco's siren call irresistible, and he had thus far refused to abandon it for anybody. Not even for his beloved Purl.

"I am trying throwing off this foul habit," Jha lied with a sneaky chuckle. "But thirty years chewing of this substance is tasting as if nectar to myself. And trees and plants here are loving it as growing fertilizer, I am informed. They are nonstop blooming, as your observings can see."

Rish wanted to fire him on the spot, but this was not the time. He must wait for the right moment before he tackled Jha.

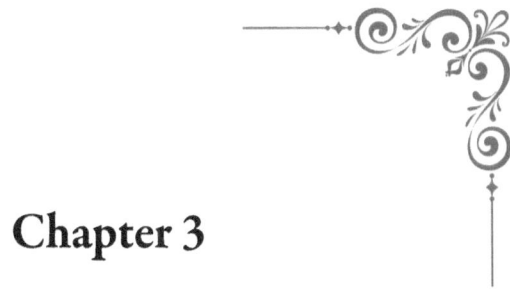

Chapter 3

Flies whizzed by in search of food scraps at the bus terminal. The humidity weighted the insects, and they twitched their forewings and stuck to the ground, witless and inert. Naini took shelter in the shade below the tin awning. She wrapped a scarf around herself against the heat and chased the flies away with the ends.

Travelers queued up at the curb, jostling for the best spots. She merged with the crowd and slipped after a family with two kids who were joining the line. The mother held her toddler daughter on her hip and the father nudged the older son ahead. He chastised the fidgety boy, clamping his arm in a firm grip. The girl stared from over her mother's shoulder, her irises as large and clear as new marbles. She flapped her chubby fingers at Naini lifting her mouth corners a tiny bit. Naini was touched by the girl's smile. She let her guard down and smiled in return.

The family hurried on and went ahead with their journey, the girl waving goodbye till she was in her seat on the bus.

Naini had slid on a pair of oversized sunglasses before she bought her fare at the ticket counter just to be cautious. The glasses disguised the upper half of her face and hid her eyes. And she did not want to be noticed or draw attention to herself today.

She studied the waiting passengers closely, observing them for telltale signs. As far as she could tell, none of the travelers at the stop resembled Lala's men in any shape or form. They looked quite normal to her, doing the things passengers do at transit stops when waiting for their rides. Teenagers bent their heads over their phones. Day laborers joked among themselves, taking digs at each other. A troupe of minstrels sang off-key, presenting their bowls for money. And monks under a tree shuffled a deck of cards with transcendental quietness. The montages were those of busy bus terminals - everyday people going where they needed to go.

Naini did not think she was tailed when she caught the auto rickshaw to get here. So maybe she was okay for now.

She was in this tight spot because two nights earlier Berto had wagered the money he borrowed from Casino Lala. When he lost it all, he accused her of prodding him into making excessive bets.

"You should have stopped me," he said.

He had griped on and on, chewing her brains as they walked home.

It was not her fault, really. She went with him on a lark, for some fun. But the good times had not rolled for Berto, and he blamed her for it. And he was still arguing with her when they reached her quarter.

He halted at a liquor store for a bottle of feni and she gave him the slip. A passing auto for hire had slowed down outside the store, and she swiftly hopped on and left. She had spent the night at the bus terminal, hatching out a plan for the morning.

Naini knew the notorious Beluga Lala, the owner of Casino Lala, would hunt for Berto when he defaulted on his loan. This was bound to happen as sure as night follows day. But the casino had seen her with him, and it was not safe for her either. Not in the city, or anywhere else in Goi for that matter. And she worried they may pursue her too. There was no telling what Lala would do.

After a sleepless night of planning, she decided she would take the morning bus to Fins Island to see her aunt. Her aunt was a housekeeper at a hotel there and Naini thought she could help her find a job at the place. It was a path out of this mess she was in, and whatever lay ahead had to be way nicer. She told herself she was going to outplay fate and come out the other side intact. As she had when she was a teen.

THE UPTURNING

Naini came from poverty, from a lineage of prostitutes living on the outskirts of a town named Satomi in Goi. She had learned to live with little right from childhood and she made do with whatever life sent her way.

The outcastes were woven into the fabric of Satomi since times past and had become part of the scenery and the history of the place. Like a familiar tree or a house one recognized and took for granted, they were simply there. A tree or a house stayed put in a spot, and so did they.

When she came of age, Naini was pledged to Daro, their deity and guardian, in a well-known custom. It was windy on the morning of the event, and the procession was on its way to the town square when the scent of sugary turnovers and fresh plumeria wafted by her. Those sweets and flowers were the traditional offerings made to Daro during the pledge ceremony. And the scents had meaning for a girl like her. It held promise. It also meant she was ready to earn a living along with the older ones.

The happy voices of women resounded in the square, and since life gave them few occasions to celebrate, their joy was infectious. For a moment she felt truly special, drunk with their admiration. She had a sense that she was not an ordinary girl playing games in the dirt anymore.

But as they swept her away something stirred inside her and smothered that spark. The rejoicing left her cold. It occurred to her that she was at the center of the festivities and yet, not really there. And that it was not about her at all. As she moved through the motions to please them, to keep their faith, to serve their purpose, the pangs passed in the noise of the ceremony.

Her mother believed her pretty daughter had excellent prospects if she bagged a wealthy patron. The celebration had brought a spot of color into her life and made her flighty. She bloomed, like a peacock with a bonus tail.

But Naini was not her mother. She was different. Born with a roving heart, she did what she wanted and went where she pleased. And so she ran off from home after the rituals to the big city of Panji and never returned. She was thirteen.

The bus driver stepped up into the vehicle. He revved the engine. A conductor punched the tickets, and they boarded. Everybody claimed their seats. The bus, its horns blaring in provocation, buffaloed its way into traffic.

A smile played on her lips as she hummed and sang.

"You and I
together as the cool waters flow by,
this is life, this is love."

It was a tune made famous by Sundari, the stunning actress in the blockbuster melodrama *River Song*. The bus drove by a billboard of the star placed high above a strip mall. Naini drank in the sight. And she daydreamed of traveling to Mumbai for a real glimpse of Sundari someday. She had seen all of her movies on the first day, first show. Even if she had to buy the tickets from a scalper for four times the box office price, she would do that without batting an eyelid. Sundari was her idol.

She felt bad for the actress who had hit a bump in her career, though. Observers predicted she was on her way out. And trade papers said the film industry was on the lookout for a fresh face. For another Sundari. Perhaps *she* could try for a bit role in a movie like the other hopefuls. And have her picture on a bigger billboard than that. Bigger than Sundari? The dizzy idea was surreal, too much. She giggled to herself to imagine it might come true.

When she got to the hotel in Vanati that afternoon, she learned her aunt had given her notice earlier that day and had left for Mumbai. No-one knew where in the large city.

She asked the receptionist at the hotel if they were hiring, and he said they had no openings, but she could try at another resort called Margosa in Bolim.

"The town is a twenty-minute bus ride from here," he told her.

Naini caught the bus to the beach town of Bolim. When she got to the resort she dawdled by the open gates, and a man weeding the flower beds noticed her standing there. He gave her a quizzical look.

"Is there any work here?" she said, calling out to him.

"Find out at the office," he said.

He waved at the front office before he wandered off with his wagon of manure.

Chapter 4

"Since when have you been up?" a drowsy Tara asked him. Sleep had filled and softened her face.

"For a while," Selvam said.

"I have to go," she said, tracing his face with a finger as she sat up.

Tara got dressed. She grabbed her tote and keys. Ready to leave, she checked her appearance in the mirror one last time. Her hair was a mess. She brushed and detangled the unruly strands and checked again. It was adequate. A quick embrace between them and she left. When she was at her desk late in the afternoon, she saw a slim woman appear at the door.

"What is it?" she asked her.

"I am looking for work," Naini said.

Besides running the weight loss clinic, Tara also managed the general upkeep of the resort. The previous day a janitor had gone off to tend to her pregnant daughter. Work on the property was lagging, and she needed someone to pick up the slack and handle maintenance.

Tara gave her an appraising look.

"Where are you from?" she asked her.

"Panji city."

"What brings you to the island?"

"The pay is more here. And they said you need workers."

Tara thought fast.

"Okay," she said. "I am low on staff, and you will have to do. There is a work shed on the property for you to stay. Jass can show you where it is. You are hired until Roopa returns."

Jass was head gardener at Margosa, and the one who guided her to the office earlier. He took Naini under his wing and led her on a tour. And he told her what she had to do on the property.

The last house on the gardener's tour was tall. A wraparound verandah with a reed sun awning encircled the lower level. Above the doorway, a jasmine vine with wanton blooms rose to the roof in all its glory.

She stared in awe. There was an identical house in the movie *Every Heart Has a Story,* the stagey seriocomedy that seized the public imagination one summer. In the scene, Rosy leans out her window to catch a butterfly flitting over flowers just like these. It was right before her graceful fall into the arms of her waiting hero below. She felt giddy, transported into a sparkly land of pretense.

"This is Rish Tilak's residence. Be sure to do a decent job here. I want no complaints," Jass said. He glanced at her to make sure she was listening.

Naini nodded. She said she understood what she must do.

Chapter 5

G*oi* Souza looked at the painting with a beady eye, perplexed why it was on the wall across from his desk. He knew it was part of a collection of Finsian tribal art. Art curated for him by a city museum. Was this one singular enough for that spot? That he did not know.

The painting showed a common rite of passage among the Kori - an island tribe. A barber was shaving an adolescent's head while his mother decorated his arms with scarlet lac. The mother's upturned gaze appeared to accuse Souza of something he could not put his finger on. Had it always been there? He remembered picking a different artwork for that spot. The terrific one of the coastal wolf hunting its prey on a mammoth dune. Whatever became of that one?

Dimwits ran his affairs, Peter Souza muttered to himself.

He must have his secretary - the only capable person in his staff - move this to storage. It was fine with him if that space stayed bare for a change. And then perhaps he might have his office quietly donate the monstrosity on the wall back to a museum - with his name as the donor.

He took a look at his schedule. A bureaucratic pastiche of dull and irrelevant meetings lay ahead. If he skipped that last appointment and went fishing at the creek instead nobody would even notice.

He could afford to take it easy. And why not? After all he had achieved plenty during his first term as Governor. He had steered the ship with skill. But because this was an election year, it brought out carping critics from all sides. The dunces did not know or care to know that winning the ballot was a breed apart. If his critics believed they could outperform him, they were welcome to try and trounce him at the polls. Fair and square. The problem was people had forgotten how his actions changed society in dramatic ways. And for the better. Take, for instance, the switch to natural gas in public buses and taxis he pushed for and passed into law. It ended pollution in the state by a third. Media groups that spewed bile at him raved when blue skies emerged in Goi. They had flung open shut windows in their gloomy press rooms and let in fresh air.

And the regulations that tied the state's bureaucrats in so many knots they had no idea if they were coming or going? His administration slashed *that* by half.

The state thrived under his 'smaller, better' economic agenda. An anti-frivolous outlay agenda that benefited residents. Voters could see that. But Goi's long drought had skewed the picture of his successes. And the squabbles over water rights with neighboring Carnak state were not helping his image either. It threw things off-kilter.

Souza refused to consider polls spun by pointy-headed news anchors. He was not that far gone yet; he had it together. None of the polls were bearers of good tidings for his party, anyway.

Still, it begged the question. Should he care about those braindead projections? He thought not. Not when it was one-sided, biased and all bad for him and the party.

His victory at the ballots depended more on how talks went with Carnak. If they came to an agreement and farms in Goi got more river water, it was a win for his party. And for him. The pollsters and their ballyhoo forecasting be damned.

A tentative knock on the door interrupted his stream of thoughts. He grimaced when his brother walked into the room. There goes my day, he said to himself.

The younger Berto was the parasite who sucked his energy. He was the millstone dragging him underwater to drown. The leech that had depleted the family of its lifeblood. Theirs was a fraught relationship, distant at its best and caustic at its worst. And when Souza had to communicate with him, he preferred his attorney do the talking.

The liverish blotches on Berto's face stood out in the harsh daylight. He wore a frayed tee, crumpled trousers, and his frowzy hair was bound with a piece of string. His beaten appearance was that of a gambler after a crushing loss.

Souza knew the purpose of his visit; he did not need to guess. His showing up like a godawful omen always concerned money. Money that he lost at the gambling table and which he did not have. Money that he spent to the second when he did have it. Berto needed a handout from him again.

"You are up early," Souza said sourly.

Berto's chin trembled with a tenuous smile. He hesitated since he meant to beg his brother for a loan. As he got his courage and pulled a chair over to grab a seat, Souza held his hand up and stopped him. His shoulders rose to his ears in a fury. His thick neck strained against his shirt collar. Berto's audacity infuriated him. It was high time he chopped the fraternal cord; a decision he should have made years earlier.

"How much did you lose?" he snapped.

Berto prepared to wheedle. He had rehearsed his lines before his visit. The words were all written up in his mind.

"I swear by our parents' graves. This is the last time I'll ask," he said, following the script.

"It will not work anymore, Berto. I am finished with you. Leave. Now."

"Please, Peter. Give me a chance. Peter, please!"

Souza called security. The guards hauled Berto outside and closed the door. And then it took another twenty minutes for him to quit the building. Berto's passive aggression had become tiresome. A cheerless Souza tried to seal off his wails, the pleading, and the insults, but the sounds pogoed off the chamber's rotunda and directly into his ears. He heard it all. He wished he never laid eyes on Berto again.

Chapter 6

Local farmers rented the towering silos on Souza farmland to store sorghum. It was a tough grain that needed little water and flourished nicely in the current drought conditions. There was a surplus this year, an upshot of a bumper yield from the earlier harvest, and the containers were filled to the brim.

This propitious scenario came with a downside. Rodents had tunneled up the soil and into the silos and were eating their way through massive quantities of grain. The contaminated product had become toxic to sell. Incensed renters fearing a catastrophe bombarded his office with complaints, and Souza promised them he would hire exterminators right away and resolve the issue. But he had run into a problem. The city's strict laws required Souza and Berto both sign off on permission forms. And Berto, being true to his nature, had skipped town.

"Well, where is he?" Vishal Batti inquired. He had served as their family lawyer for more years than either of them remembered.

Souza was still seething with residual anger. He shifted with impatience when he heard the question. Berto was history to him after that last clash between them. It was the definitive straw which broke their bond, and he was in no mood for explanations.

"Who the hell knows!" he said, glowering at the lawyer. "He left my office days ago screaming obscenities at me."

"Have you reached out to him?" Batti asked him.

"My staff has. But he is gone, fallen off the face of the earth. Do we really need his consent for pest control?"

"Under the current laws, we do. Once he turns up, we can draw up papers and split your assets. For the meantime protect the grain. Or you will have bigger complications on your hands."

"My guys are doing just that! They have concealed bait near the silos. Hidden traps and stuff."

"Did it work?"

"With mixed results. The fiends are devious.

"Ah. The Goyan rat is intrepid, I am told."

"And wily to boot. They can sniffle out lures from miles."

Souza rotated a paperweight on his desk and contemplated the state of his affairs. This was an unnecessary distraction. He wanted things on a steady keel until the upcoming elections, but he had a hodgepodge of problems flying at him. Farmers held daily protests outside the Statehouse, his official seat. They clamored for more water for their dying farms. The previous week's talks among the states had failed again and farmers blamed him for the failure. And now, this.

His campaign for reelection was on a slippery slide. Another misstep, and it could all go downhill for him.

"I can send Jiva Kelkar out to find him. He owes me a personal favor," Souza said, looking moodily at him.

"Ah, yes!" murmured Batti. "The Zigzag case guy. He has a dodgy record."

Two petty thieves called Zig and Zag caused a sensation one festival season. The crooks robbed a string of jewelry shops downtown and then had fled with the loot. Leads and clues culled by police led nowhere. Business sank; stores went bankrupt. When desperate owners demanded action from the police commissioner, he assigned his best detective to the case.

"You remember that one?" Souza said.

"The festival season that set off shop alarms daily," Batti replied wryly.

"He set a thief to catch a thief."

"Sharp work. But questionable tactics."

"The two *were* thieves."

"He rounded up Zig's old parents like they were criminals. A blatant flouting of Section 277 of the Penal Code."

"Pfft! They were Zig's weak point, and he exploited it," Souza said with a laugh.

"He confiscated his pets without a warrant."

"The pets should have resisted and asked for one."

Batti looked pained by the joke.

"Did you watch the viral video of the parakeet?" Souza asked.

"I did not," Batti replied.

"But you should have. The bird could cuss up a storm. It was hilarious."

"The bird died."

"And has gone to a better place. Lighten up, Batti!"

"What about the endangered Mudhol hounds?"

"The dogs were bought at a thieves' market of exotic animals. So was the parakeet. Both acts are felonious animal-cruelty crimes."

"He pretended he had Zag in custody."

"And he pointedly thanked him for the tip on Zig on primetime news. A genius move!" Souza said amusedly.

After the airing of that show, Kelkar had reaped what he sowed. Some good, and some not-so-good. When a livid Zig received wind of the news, he thought Zag had ratted him out. He folded like a cheap suit and fessed up. Police took the thieves into custody and the jewelry merchants wiped their brows in relief. That was the good part. The bad part was that Zig's elderly parents landed in the hospital from the stress. And the media had a field day blaming him.

The department heads put Kelkar through a grilling, had a publicized hearing and the whole nine yards, but he was a hero by then. Meanwhile, Zig's relatives recovered and went home. At the hearing's close, top brass decided his methods had brought fugitives to justice in any case. He escaped with a mere reprimand.

Batti puckered his face.

"This could be politically risky," he said.

"Every damn thing is," Souza said. He picked up his phone.

"Get me Jiva Kelkar on my private line," he said to his secretary at the other end.

Chapter 7

"Hot chai, Ferdy. And make it quick. I leave in fifteen minutes," he said to Ferdy, his admin.

This would be Kelkar's fifth cup of tea this morning. There were no more amnesiac nights for him once he picked up the habit. He woke up at home every day.

Ferdy was alone in the office, watching a live American football match on his computer. It was the last, and potentially winning play of the quarter. A nail-biting finish lay ahead. The quarterback, in the ultimate game of his career, had the ball in his possession. He was poised for a doable five-yard throw.

Ferdy sighed when he heard Kelkar. He hit mute and changed tabs to the department's homepage right away.

"One chai coming up," Ferdy said, acting jaunty.

He logged off and scampered to the cafe across the street for some tea.

Kelkar had put his routine cases on the back burner after talking with the Governor. He made Berto his top priority.

Souza contended that Berto must be found before the elections. There was no other option. If the rodent matter exploded in public before then it would affect the vote. As things were, farmers doubted his negotiation skills. The bloc viewed him with suspicion. If a trifling crisis blew up and became unmanageable, he could lose a whole voting bloc.

THE UPTURNING

Remembrance of an old debt he owed Souza forced his hand, and he agreed to accept the case. Souza's problem fell onto his lap and was his problem now.

He scrutinized the photograph of Berto posing with Deni Shood, the owner of Local & Foreign Spirits. The two besties leered at the camera in chummy fashion with arms draped over each other.

He recollected that Deni was a sometime drug dealer cited years ago for selling imported liquor with no permit. They raided his store for evidence, but Deni's mob friends pressured witnesses who recanted their testimony. The case got tossed and he squirmed out of a stint in jail. Punishment had deflected from him like water off a duck's tail.

Ferdy deposited a fresh cup of tea on his desk.

Kelkar sipped the mulled brew and stared at the horizon's line. A million inquisitive people lived in Goi, and somebody out there had the information he needed. He prepared to seize the day.

Chapter 8

Local & Foreign Spirits had arguably the best selection of liquor in the capital. But some liquors were more special than others.

Premium vodka reigned supreme among all foreign spirits at the store. The bottles flew off the racks in hours. East European drug dealers who came as tourists to Goi and stayed were the biggest buyers. Nobody checked them, not for years. And shifty bar owners like Deni smuggled the expensive contraband via gulf sea pirates and sold it by the pallet to the dealers. Deni had gotten rich with these under-the-table dealings. His business was good.

And then there was feni, the favorite in the local section. Goyans drank feni on festive occasions or for no reason at all. The fermented cashew drink had a flavor and aroma not for the faint of heart. If you enjoyed the stinging brew, you wanted to be stung more. But if you drank to oblivion or on an empty stomach, it rendered a kick you remembered well the next morning. No middle ground existed with feni. You were a fan, or you were not.

Chimes sounded as Kelkar walked in through the door. The salesclerk at the store was running a duster over the bottle tops. He missed spots but he seemed to neither care nor notice.

"Where is your boss?" Kelkar asked him.

The clerk looked up at him with a trained blandness. He began to speak but shut up at once. His gaze had slithered to the far end of the room and again to Kelkar. A hirsute man in a partway buttoned shirt and metallic jeans had stepped through the curtain panels slung at the back of the room. The man was Deni Shood, the proprietor, and Berto's buddy from the photograph. He smirked when Kelkar held up his badge.

"How can I help?" Deni said, touching his forehead in mock salute.

Kelkar slid a photograph on the counter.

"Seen this man?" he said.

"Sure," Deni said, not missing a beat. He had a look that was even blander than his employee. "That's Berto. The G's brother."

"I hear he is a regular."

"He is. Have not seen him lately, though."

"Call the Panji station if he turns up."

"There are dangerous men after Berto.

"Who is?"

"Beluga Lala is looking for him, too."

"You jerking the police around?"

Deni pulled back, feigning outrage.

"Why would I do that?" he protested smarmily, with his hand on his heart.

"Tell me what I don't know."

Deni's soft smirk returned and stuck. Kelkar pointed at the vodka bottles winking under the lights.

"Got a license to sell all that fancy vodka?" he asked Deni.

When Deni lifted his shoulders in an elaborate shrug, Kelkar swept his arm over the merchandise and knocked them. The bottles shattered into pieces on the warm tiled floor and the alcohol steamed upward in wisps.

A homeless man outside the storefront was pushing a shopping cart piled high with his life's worth. The commotion made him stop and stare into the store. He gathered something was afoot when he saw Deni in the center of the wrecked shop, his jaws open like a gasping fish. The man leaned raffishly on his cart, entertained by the spectacle.

Kelkar snatched two bottles of expensive Goyan port from the shelf and gave it to him.

"Free for you, with compliments of Mr. Deni Shood here," he said to the man.

The surprised man took the bottles.

Deni shouted in alarm and rushed toward the door. The homeless fellow correctly understood he must make a quick getaway if he wanted to keep the free stuff. He pressed his rattling haulage forward in a rush.

A tawny cat that was hiding under a blanket in the cart panicked at the noise and clambered to the roof, hissing at him all the way up. He cajoled his pet for a moment but was more intent on leaving before Deni caught up with him.

"I'll come for you later, Mondo," the man yelled over his shoulder as he fled the scene.

Deni hopped across the floor in his pursuit of the man. Fifteen bottles of his absolutely premium vodka were crushed to smithereens. His attention was so fixed on Kelkar, he almost tripped over the clerk clearing the mess on the floor.

"Have a lovely day, Deni," Kelkar said with a grin. He drove away from the curb.

Deni was struck speechless by the cop. His first thought was to file a grievance and recoup his damages. This is preposterous, he said to the clerk, reaching for his phone. His second thought overruled the first. He had run the store on an expired permit for the past year. That latter thought sobered him fast, and he decided to take the loss and let the problem slide.

He got to the entrance of the store, and a longtime client coming in greeted him, but Deni waved him aside without so much as a peep in his direction. The visit from the cop had left him frazzled.

Chapter 9

The police chief swept red tape aside when he heard of his assignment. Xavier Rego, a newbie, was moved from desk to active duty and made his deputy within a day.

"We are on the right street, sir. Turn left by that beggar at the street corner," Rego said, watching street signs as they cruised through the business district.

Stocky and quick with a smile, Rego knew every lane in the sooty city. He was a walking, talking map. Many of the streets had posts missing, and some were weathered beyond recognition, but he located addresses just the same. He seemed to enjoy navigating these cramped spaces.

The grease sluiced out of gutters by a downpour varnished the roads. Light from stores shimmered on oily puddles of rainwater on the tar. People thronged about the shambolic food carts in the city's commercial district where food was cooking on enormous skillets. They ate, paid, and left, and were replaced in an instant by another hungry group who ate, paid, and left. The cook never paused, not even to wipe his damp face. He scraped, fried, and turned in continuous motion and piled meats and greens on plate after plate. A sprig of cilantro, a fork on the top, and he dished them out to each buyer over the counter.

It was rich hearty fare for the frugal and the poor.

The lit office buildings and cars at curbs said workers were still at their desks. All along the crisscross of lanes separating the skyscrapers were a mélange of vintage shops. The workday had ended for the shop owners who pulled down the metal doors and padlocked them. They darted, their cellphones pasted to their ears, leather pouches with holding straps wrapped around their wrists. It was a uniform, an unwitting fashion statement affected by merchants in the district. And one easily identified them by their clothing and accouterments.

Once they left the poky streets behind, they entered a dark alley that was bordered with shuttered store exits on either hand.

"You mentioned a landmark earlier," Kelkar said.

"The pigeon circle coming up ahead," Rego said.

He rolled by a park fenced with a manicured hedge. In the park, a lone man stood on a stone platform that had once supported a Portuguese colonel's statue. He was throwing handfuls of bird seed up into the sky at starved thrushes. The birds swarmed about him, slapping him with wings and staining his clothes with their droppings. He smiled from ear to ear as they went by him. Kelkar shook his head in bemusement. The city was strange at night.

Rego showed him the little shrine built within a banyan tree's extensive roots. And then more stores.

"Past the shrine," he said. "Past the pawn shops on your left. And there it is."

There was a fluorescent sign on the brick frontage that said '*Casino Lala.*' Drunken couples stumbled through a side door, blinked in the light and fell helplessly over cars double-parked for blocks. A cluster of women in sequined dresses and glossed lips teetered on pencil heels at the corner, adding a touch of glitz to the quarter.

The main entrance had scalpers conducting a brisk but discreet sale of tickets. Loan sharks handed out money to overdrawn gamblers like free candy. And loud customers denied entry for one reason, or another tried every brazen trick in the trade to get in. The entire place had the gaudy energy of a fly-by-night, shady carnival.

Lala's casinos fronted as gambling dens, while he ran cash laundering operations in their back offices. It was here that businesses with illegal funds came for help. His primary occupation involved turning their black money white.

Although dressed in sporty khakis and cotton shirts, their bearing gave them away much before they arrived at the doors. Muscly bouncers who guarded the entrance exchanged looks with each other as if to say there may be trouble ahead. The bouncers moved aside and let them in but eyed their backs with a watchful unease.

Gamblers were playing hard at the tables inside, and the lookers-on betted on who would survive a round, goading them like crowds cheering on gladiators and lions in the arena. It was a sport in itself.

They passed the gamblers and cut through the haze of cigarette smoke in the room. On an upraised stage, pouting dancers wearing satiny blouses and skirts swiveled their hips and glided to disco music. Kelkar had a closer glimpse at their faces, and it shocked him to see how young they were.

They cleared past the rowdy drinkers at the bar and reached a solitary door at the corridor's end. They walked into the room. Beluga Lala reclined on an overstuffed sofa with his bare feet propped on a padded stool. A spindly boy was seated opposite him on the floor, gingerly dabbing a tinctured swab on Lala's feet.

"Welcome to my lair, detective," Lala said with a brassy laugh. He had recognized Kelkar from his previous run-ins with vice.

Lala broke laws with a rude daring because he had a network of cops under his control who took his money and did his bidding. Charges filed against him at dawn got dropped at the end of the day or soon after.

Lala's comfort in his surroundings, and his own embarrassment at the corruption inbred in the force, set off Kelkar. This was a criminal who bribed his way out of jail for offenses he continued to commit. Lala belonged in a cell among beasts worse than him. Kelkar marched to the stool and kicked it from under Lala.

"Stand up, sonofabitch," he erupted.

The frightened boy released Lala's foot and flew out the room.

"I mean no disrespect, but I cannot," Lala blustered.

He struggled to stand. Scabrous blisters dotted his soles and oozed blood.

"Where is Berto Souza?"

"My men are looking for him, too!"

"You will land in Arawad jail yesterday if anything happens to him."

"The bastard owes me a chunk of cash."

"Si Tabela is serving time there now. You two can get reacquainted. Have a playdate."

The prospect of being in the same prison as his nemesis, Si Tabela, a felon accused of murder in several states, stirred up a fear in Lala. The perspiration dribbled down his jowls and onto his shirt. They shared an ancient enmity, the hoodlum's kind. The sort that would drag on for the rest of their lifespans.

"Who did Berto come with?" Kelkar asked, his tone casual.

Lala patted away the sweat.

"A woman with cat eyes. He cussed at her when he lost, as if she were to blame," he said.

"By the way, your bar dancers are juveniles. Do you grab them from schools now?"

Lala hobbled to the sofa and sank into the cushions to nurse his tender feet. He dripped sheer venom.

When they got out of the fusty confines of the casino, he tossed the car keys at Rego.

"Drive us to Borani's. I am in the mood for *bun maska* and chai. You know the way, I presume," he said.

"I can get there blindfolded."

"Eyes open, Rego. We have had plenty of excitement for today."

The circular café was furnished with pleather chairs and thick wood tables. One side of the café had a row of carved doorways that opened onto the busy thoroughfare. On the spotty walls between the doors were laminated photos of bygone celebrities. A distinct eggy smell came from the chalky paint and percolated through but faded and became part of the air the longer you sat there.

Borani's was far livelier during the day when college students came for a sugar rush from the café's cream cakes and flaky pastries. After dark, chain-smoking night owls packed the café and surfed the net for hours in a strung-out silence. They pecked at their food and whispered into their phones like shadowy government operatives on a top-secret mission. The loners had an odor about them as they went past, something separate from what was in the room, an odor of burnt toast and mothballs.

Everybody in town knew Rustomji, the flamboyant owner of the café. He was a fixture at the cash register until he closed at two in the morning, and he could be heard no matter where you sat. He never ran out of stories, and he regaled regulars stopping by with off-color jokes that had them busting their sides with laughter. His ramblings were always about him and one of the dead celebs in the picture frames. Timepass, he called it.

Kelkar bit into the buttery bun that had a warm-off-the-oven yeastiness. Pieces of candied fruit in its fluff lent it a delicious crunch. He washed the sweetness of the bread down with sips of hot cinnamon-laced tea.

Rego dug into an omelet sandwich with a side of pumpkin ketchup. They discussed their leads.

"What do you think of the case?" he asked Rego.

"It is puzzling how Berto has vanished," Rego said.

"People disappear for no reason. By accident or by design. It is an irritant for police too."

"He has to surface someday, right?"

"When he runs out of time or money."

"Maybe we can catch up to him before he makes a mess."

"His type often does. What did you learn from our informants?"

"No news from the streets, yet. I checked on all his familiar haunts, but he has not shown up for a while."

"We must stop at Navigaon terminal next. Rule out the possibility he hopped on a bus to some place. They are the cheapest means to travel."

Thousands of travelers breezed through the terminal each day. And there was a decent chance somebody remembered Berto even though days had flown by.

"I meet with Exit tomorrow," Rego said. "He is our last remaining informant and could have a report for us."

"Let's look into the terminal once you are done with him. The trail has run cold in Goi - unless we hear otherwise from Exit or witnesses there. Fins Island is a hop, step, and jump away. The island cops are laidback. And it is the only island in these parts with heaps of tourists. My guess is the girl is headed there. If we find her, I am certain we can find Berto."

"And if we do not?"

"We search inland."

Rego slipped a tip for the waiter under the paper receipt. They waved to Rustomji who locked the restaurant doors after them and switched off the lights.

Outside, a moist, smoky breeze blew by, brushing them like a spritz of fragrance.

Stores had shut for the night, and the food trucks had drifted elsewhere, leaving everything empty. Homeless slept in rows on the sidewalk, their bodies huddled together under threadbare sheets. And naked infants slumbered in bliss between the families with tiny hands curled into their palms as if they held a fond toy.

Downtown was winding down a few hours before daybreak. A brief letup before the city bounded to life again.

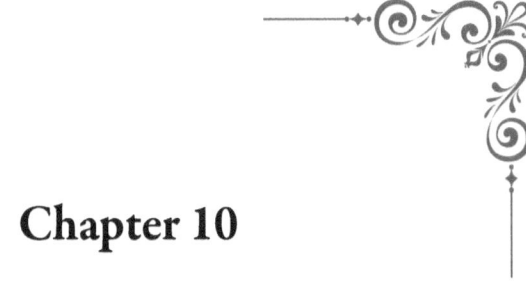

Chapter 10

The words 'Happy Birthday Mini' written in lights flashed and faded over the roof. His daughter Mini turned sixteen that day, and Lala had organized an extravagant party for the joyous occasion. The party was a who's who of guests, and he greeted the rich and famous coming in at the door and ushered them to the lawn.

Under a marquee in the courtyard, a brass band teased out music for the adults. Children dressed in silk ran between the servers who were balancing trays of food held high. The little ones plonked themselves on the grass and gorged on sweets stamped with Mini's picture.

After the band packed up and left, a concert by the famous superstar CC was to come next. He had a legion of teen fans and Mini was one among them. The concert was going to be the highlight of the night.

Lala had forked out a good amount of cash for the private concert. And the brash, showy party suited Lala; it was to his taste. An ecstatic Mini blew thankful flying kisses at him, which he acknowledged with an indulgent nod and a toothy grin in her direction. She was the light of his life. How the years had flown! In an abnormal second of melancholy for him, he wished he could slow time and keep her the way she was a little longer.

The youthful audience could not wait for their hero's act, and a wave of excitement rose and fluttered through the throng. They shot up from their seats, their lifted faces shiny with rapture.

It was near midnight when the limousine carrying CC, and his entourage appeared. His makeup and ensemble team switched off their phones and rushed to the gates. The crew closed around him and bundled him away to a trailer in Lala's backyard where they fussed at his appearance for a stretch.

Soon after, psychedelic lights skated over the heads of screaming onlookers. The actor, every inch a megastar, sprang onto the platform. His gelled hair was iridescent, slick. He wore reflective sunglasses, a glitter suit, and his shoes tapered to impossible points. When he struck a pose right out of one of his blockbuster movies, it was too much for Mini and her friends to bear. They screamed for joy, broke down, and hugged each other.

The star grooved to his fan favorite tunes, and he changed his outfits, hairstyles and dapper hats several times, dazzling them. Then he kneeled and extended his arm out to the blushing. birthday girl. She slipped her hand into his and stepped on the stage. They danced to a slow number. CC stayed his usual chill self, but Mini was in an advanced state of delirium.

The stage rocked with hit after hit of his songs. An hour went by, and another. All was well until a sudden glitch in the sound system warped the music. The song wound down into an agonizing slow spiral and stopped with a blowout of static. Partygoers booed. The frustrated star quit his dancing, and he jumped offstage for a cold brew. While he waited for technicians to remedy the malfunction, his makeup crew daubed his upper lip with a powder puff and retouched his face. One of them fed him softy ice cream in a giant cone.

The event was rapidly becoming a non-event. A rightly upset Lala did not want Mini and her friends let down on her special day. And he immediately sent two of his men, Tips Sattu and Ludi Rodriguez, to fix the hitch. Tips went to talk to the star, but when he got closer to him, he noted something irregular about the celluloid prince.

THE UPTURNING

At their home, his daughter Bina replayed CC videos on their big screen TV till everybody pleaded with her to stop. And Tips had watched the same song and romp sequences, albeit with reluctance, on countless occasions. He took a certain pride in remembering a person's oddities.

Right off the bat, Tips thought the star's eyebrows were too black and thick. They looked fake to him, more penciled unibrow than the natural winged beauties on screen. And his ears stuck out a mile. Like those of a stern marsupial on guard duty. A doubting Tips narrowed his eyes at the star. His pointed look made CC uncomfortable, and he pulled out his phone and began a pretend conversation with nobody at the other side. The panicky ploy did not fool Tips. It had him staring even harder at the puddling guest of honor.

Tips concluded that the performer in front of him differed from the one in the videos. This was a masquerader, a doppelgänger, a faker. A nasty, no-good fraud who dared fool credulous girls, including his daughter Bina. An angry Tips hurried to Lala.

"There is *dal mein kuch kaala*, Lala*ji*. Soup has black pebble in it, sir," he said to him, moving his eyeballs from end to end.

"Make yourself clear, Tips," Lala said, looking vacant.

He did not like the folksy proverbs Tips bandied about when grave matters were at hand. Besides, metaphors in general mystified him. They bounced over his head.

"That is not CC," Tips said, disturbed by the star's betrayal.

"You are trying my patience, Tips."

"He is a lookalike, Lala*ji*."

"Where is the original?"

"I know not, Lala*ji*. I am confused too."

"What are you waiting for? Find out!"

While the sound remained down, the imposter kept himself busy by clicking solo selfies from every angle possible. He understood the jig was up when he saw Tips and Ludi scowling at him.

They held him by his elbows and herded him into an empty room. The flustered duplicate named Savor claimed innocence. He said the real CC was in the middle of reshooting a movie's climax he had botched earlier. And he sent him in his place because they were facsimiles of each other. The irate movie director would boycott him and end his career if he missed the shoot, and he promised Savor a generous cut if he performed at the bash and pretended to be him.

Savor went on and on in that vein, tripping over himself, until they got the idea. When they told Lala about what had happened, the casino owner lost his temper.

"Where is Chocolate Candy?" he demanded.

"He is on a shoot in Fins Island," they said.

"Go drag him by his mane and bring him here. This carbon copy must dance for his life until his arrival. He is dead if my Mini finds out."

"Yes, sir*ji*."

The word chocolate triggered Lala. It set his taste buds on fire.

"And bring me some of that island dessert you rave about," he said to Tips.

"Wah, Lala*ji*! Wow. You are blessed with admirable memory!" Tips said appreciatively.

"Baa, bee, boo something."

"Close, sir*ji*. It is called bebintia."

"Yes, that one."

"Double order, Lala*ji*? Serving size is small."

"Make it four."

The film crew was sixty miles away on the island, and Tips and Ludi raced across the capital and threatened the director until he gave in. They brought the star to Lala.

"You perform for the girls, Chocolate boy," Lala said to him, his eyes bloodshot. He did not get why Mini thought this bottom feeder a hero. But what did he know about being cool.

THE UPTURNING

The authentic CC completed the show to the young crowd's satisfaction. And the radiant girls posted a gazillion pictures to social media, never suspecting Lala had averted a major birthday crisis. Their merrymaking continued as planned.

After the night's upheavals, Lala and his partners retired to relax and have a drink.

Once he got a moment alone with Max Sing, an associate of his who owned a nationwide trucking business, they chewed the fat awhile.

They knew each other from their early years in a heartless city. When every night, poor and starving, they had returned to the decrepit underpass they called home. The shared hardship of that sorry past made Lala trust him the most from all the others in his coterie.

"There is a bit of a situation," he confided to Sing. "The Guvnor's brother owes me money."

"A good thing."

"There is a problem. A cop's dealing with the case now."

"What can a cop do?" Sing, who transacted regularly with corrupted cops, said.

"My men are on the brother's trail. But I am not sure if he is worth the trouble."

"Word spreads you let go a debt, then you will have actual trouble. Do what you got to do, Lala."

"The bastard must repay me. I am not letting him off that easy."

"Go tell that to his brother. Politicians hate the wrong kind of publicity. Trust me, he will wish it disappeared fast."

Lala, who enjoyed twisting arms, stroked his chin and said that he may do just that. Sing had put ideas in his head. Why send men all over Goi in search of a broke louse when he could badger the loaded family and get results faster, he thought.

His associates left, and his men brought in the day's records for Lala to examine. He tallied the proceeds and handed them directives.

After they finished, he poured himself a finger of his finest scotch.

"What about the girl?" he asked Tips.

"I heard she is from the city," Tips said.

"Find her. And Berto. I want my cash back."

"No worries, Lala*ji*. He cannot do *paani men rehkar magarmach se bair*," Tips said in ominous tones.

"What does that mean, anyhow?" Lala said, annoyed once more.

"It means you cannot live in watery abode and make crocodile your enemy."

"I do not like it when you talk in riddles, Tips. Who is the crocodile?"

Lala did not follow. The subtleties of language had eluded him again. And he wondered if Tips was mocking him.

"Lala*ji*, I assert you are ridiculously enormous crocodile. Berto is nothing," Tips said in all sincerity, soothing troubled waters.

The explanation placated Lala. He lay back into the settee. A crocodile, indeed. He waved Tips aside and ordered him to hurry on with the job of finding Berto.

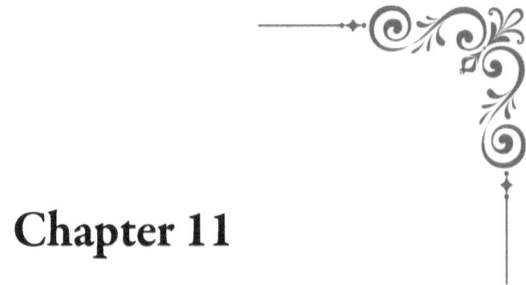

Chapter 11

ins Island

F   On Fridays, the two of them bought half-priced tickets to the matinee at a downtown theater. They watched from the trashy front rows and ate oily samosas and fries with necks craned far back on the headrests. Naini loved musicals. And she danced in her seat at the song sequences happening every ten minutes in the three-hour long show. Berto didn't care one way or another. He was quite happy to be in an air-conditioned room and out of the sweltering heat outside, and he slept off and on till the show came to an end.

One night after a late screening, she went home while he caught up with Deni Shood for a round of drinks at a local casino. They had to walk through the modish gaming rooms to get to the bar. The action at the tables was multiplied ten-fold by the mirrors on the walls, and Berto was captivated by the sleight of hands of gamblers hoping for a bit of luck. He wanted a piece of that glitzy life. Be a somebody in that world.

After the meetup with Deni, if he had any money at all, he went to the casino and gambled it away. It thrilled him when the riotous floor announced the winners. Sirens blared; bells rang. The elation of the gamers was something to behold. He went to the tables like a horse with blinkers on, not seeing those who sank under their losses.

On that night at Casino Lala, she was all dressed up in her finest clothes. She sparkled with excitement at each spin of the roulette. The overhead lights glinted off her olive eyes as she smiled, and the play of colors reminded him of the time they first met.

To distract himself, he talked big of making a sweep at the betting station. He was going to strike it rich tonight, he said to her. It made Naini laugh. Her laughter irritated him, and so he went all out and bet everything he had. That would teach her, he thought.

At each turn, the ball shot a number forward of his pick with spooky regularity. This happened so often he was convinced the wheel had evil notions of its own. But he could not stop, and his shortfalls spun into a running joke at the table.

Her gaze drifted toward the exit.

When his cash was gone, he borrowed an advance from the house for a final wager. Casino management recognized him. They agreed to lend him the cash only because of his connection with the Governor. The loan came attached with a steep interest - a minor thing he overlooked. Flush with the house's funds, he wagered it all. And by closing hour, he had squandered every last chip.

He missed the initial installment, which was due the next morning, and so Lala dispatched his men after him. Lala was feared and loathed in Goi with good reason. His ruthlessness, that he had police in his pocket, fortified his power and made him dangerous. Only the insane trifled with Lala.

Berto was afraid for his life by now, and he fled underground. Then days afterward, while he was still hiding, Deni sent him a frantic warning. He said a city detective was looking for him too. Berto had not the faintest clue as to why a cop was interested in him. He was certain it was a simple case of mistaken identity. Lala's reach once he acted petrified him more than anything, and so he blanked out the entire cop episode.

He blamed Naini for everything. His losses were her fault, and he went to find her just so he could tell her that. When he swung by her lean-to, new tenants had already shifted into the shabby dwelling. The tenants were up and about unloading their belongings from splintery wood crates. Overwrought, he collapsed at the front door, feeling as helpless as a newborn pup. Neighbors who picked up his cries gathered around him, and one of them tipped him off about Naini's aunt. The aunt was her only living relative, she said.

He got his thoughts together. It was obvious that Lala's sway over Goi was unshakeable. His cronies thrived in places where bribery had a hold. Berto knew all that. He also knew if he valued his life, the wisest choice was to put more distance between them. The island was a superb stopgap location. He spent many summers there as a child, and he knew each nook and cranny. If he escaped there for a period and hid out, it might remove him from Lala's crosshairs. At least for a while.

On his way to the bus terminal, thirsty for a drink, he stopped at an illicit liquor store and ordered a bottle of their cheapest hooch. The questionable alcohol was a noxious third-rate brand favored by poor miserables, but this was all he could afford these days. He drank, wallowing and festering till he finished the bottle.

At the platform, he lurched to the ticketing booth and bought a ticket. He aired his problems to anybody who cared to listen, and he began to create a scene. When the clerks at the counter ordered him to get moving or they would notify the cops, he left in a hurry to catch his bus.

The 11 pm Final was the last bus to the island and was about to exit Navigaon terminal. A drunk Berto shinnied up the steps, and he squeezed into a narrow spot at the rear. Passengers with small animals in wicker baskets crammed the state-run night bus, and the enclosed space was steamy and fetid. The ride along the potholed road jarred and knocked his head against the hard seat but did not wake him. His ordeal had exhausted him.

When they landed on the island, the driver shook him awake. He told him to step off the bus. A bleary Berto gazed around and realized he was the only passenger on board. The bus dropped him off and departed for the return journey, taking its light with it. Bit by bit the red taillights disappeared out of sight and his surroundings changed to a pitch black.

The tide roared from ahead. Disoriented by the dark, he inched toward the sounds of the sea. He halted at the line of shorefront trees at the rim of the beach. Whitecaps rolled over submerged rocks and smashed onto the sands. A luminescence shone on the crashing waters, and the foamy crests of the waves were like ghostly birds having a midnight frolic. He wanted to wade in and swim with them, but he was too tired to move.

A stone's throw from where he stood, a bonfire burned by the water's edges. A stick-like man and a woman with a bulky bag beside her sat near the fire. The gaunt man reached for the bag, and he plucked out rolls of cash from the inside. Berto observed them drowsily until he could no longer. Then he rested against a tree trunk and fell into a deep sleep.

He awoke midmorning to find the shore uninhabited. Pieces of scorched driftwood, remnants from the previous night's bonfire, lay scattered on the sand. He swam into the sea and dove under. The mix of grit and brine scratched at his throat, and as he bobbed on a wave, his thirst worsening, he ogled the restaurants on the beach with envy. Waiters set chairs and tables on the garden terraces and opened the patio umbrellas for customers who picnicked in the sunshine. He hungered for a plate of fried fish, a glass of cashew feni. The spirit's kick would knock out the whirr in his mind and help him think of a plan to save himself.

Chapter 12

G *oi*

The next morning, Tips and Ludi barged into Naini's former neighborhood with enough gasoline in their car to light up the hovels. Old timers at the slum recognized the thugs and knew their visit meant mayhem. They warned the rest before fleeing inside and locking their front doors.

When tenants ignored the loud knocks, Tips splashed a gallon jug of the fuel over the cardboard shanties. He threatened to burn the entire place to ashes. Every pair of frightened ears in the vicinity heard his threats. The adults bunched up in the wall corners with children in arms and their scared families. Parents patted round little heads, promising them that the men would leave soon, and said all would be well again.

The cries of small children too young to be reassured came from the interiors, and the screams added to the chaos. One brave individual rushed out in spite of the warnings.

"She does not live here anymore," he cried. He backed out the alley and told them Naini had gone to see her aunt.

Ludi charged at the man who scampered up a tall fence and vanished before he got within a few feet of him. Tips commanded the situation. In a parting shot, he talked of dire consequences if anybody snitched on Lala.

"Don't be saying *aa bail mujhe maar* to Beluga Lala," he yelled.

"You heard him. Asking whale to come and hit you is foolish," Ludi shouted out.

"Ox, not whale," Tips corrected him.

"Asking ox, not whale, to come and hit you is foolish," Ludi said.

"Nice work, Ludi. Let's go," Tips said with a sigh.

And armed with the information, the hoodlums left.

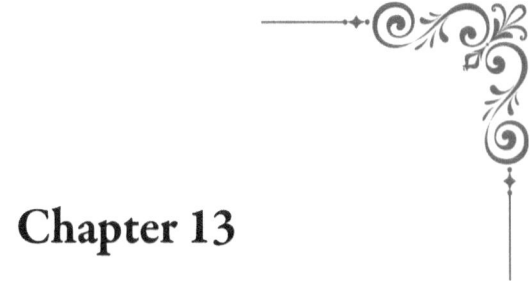

Chapter 13

Fins Island
    Naini stood by a pipal tree on the path ahead and he slowed to watch her. She drew her braid over her shoulder and knotted it into a coil at her nape. Filmy sunlight streamed through the branches, rimming her face and figure. The glass bangles at her slender wrists sparked like jewels and clinked as she moved. Rish walked past and around the corner, the sounds echoing in his ears as he took the stairs up to the family room.

"The retreat guests are here, I noticed," Mira remarked as he stepped into the room.

"They begin their schedule tomorrow," he said.

"Governor Souza will be here in the morning with his entourage. I thought you should know. Though it may be a bother for the guests, I do not expect him to stay long," she said.

She appeared engaged as she organized her papers and stuffed letters into envelopes. He started a motion to leave.

"I do not see you anymore," she said, looking up at him.

The trace of complaint in her voice escaped his attention. As always in their interactions with each other, words only widened the gulf between them.

"The resort keeps me busy. Is all well with you?"

"I have the usual aches that age brings. Who does not?"

"Should I send for Dr. Mali?"

"It is not important. A good night's sleep is the medicine," she said. Testy, she waved him away.

Chapter 14

B ir rolled up bamboo shades on the wide glass wall, and the early rays of the sun trickled in and warmed the studio. There were six of them who had signed up for the retreat. Claudia and Herb Rumbler were the first ones in. Vikki Mesa rushed in next thinking she was late for class.

"Am I late?" she asked Sandy Tauno who was laying her mat on the wood floor.

"We haven't started yet," Sandy said.

"My quads are super tight," Greg Bilisk who had just come in said. He stretched up on his toes.

"Yeah, mine too. The studio looks great," Vikki said, looking around.

"It's a nice space for yoga. Lots of light," Claudia said.

They made more small talk and introduced themselves.

The last one in was Pravesh Doss who slouched in silently and stared out the windows.

Minutes before the session, Bir showed them the blocks, bolsters, straps, and blankets arranged on shelves and the group picked up what was needed. The handy props in reach, they settled onto the mats on the hardwood floor.

He began by singing a devotional ode to Patanjali, the seer of yoga. They stayed still with palms held together in Anjali mudra, the prayer gesture, in a salute to their innermost light. And their breath deepened and expanded in the following quiet.

The active session started, and the group flowed from one asana, from one posture to the next. He tugged a leg here, steadied a quaky arm there. When he came to the women made unsteady by the demands of a twisty pose, he straddled their hips to realign muscle and bone. He hovered near them until he became warm.

At the end of the session a sweet rejuvenation arrived with Savasana - the corpse position. They stopped all doing and lay like corpses, their limbs heavy, and they gave in to the pull of the earth. The tired ones among them let go of everything and fell asleep the minute they lay down. A good quarter hour of relaxation later, a bell tone stirred them awake. Refreshed, they sat up. They folded up their mats and put the props back on the shelves. The studio emptied.

Bir changed into his sweats. And he set out for a sight of Paroma, his current crush at the front office, with his heart on his sleeve.

Chapter 15

A broad sweep of turf stretched from the resort to a low retaining wall at the beach line. Vikki chose a spot in the shade and placed a mat on the lawn. She had come down to the beach to take in the sunset. It was another fine day on the island. The vast endless ocean coruscated under the setting sun. A whisper of a breeze caressed her skin as she sat motionless for a while with her eyes closed. Evening hours were her favorite time. The sultry day had softened at the edges with the coming of dusk and the light was mellow.

She opened her eyes, and the first thing she saw was Sandy strolling at the tide's edge. Sandy waded in with her sandals in hand and with her trousers rolled up at the ankles. Her bare feet quashed through the sand and the rippling waves as she made her way across the beach. The pushy hawkers selling cheap sarongs followed her and asked if she wanted to try one on. When Sandy showed no interest in buying, the hawkers wandered off and left her alone.

Vikki watched a thin stick-like man with streaky dreadlocks and a woman in a long dress come in from an access road. The man's strides were wide, and it was apparent he knew this space well. His partner, in a sharp contrast to him, loitered steps behind. The group of hawkers who were aggressive moments before scattered as soon as the couple came closer and disappeared. Their unexpected appearance, and a certain oddness they had, made Vikki hold her breath in anticipation.

Sandy stopped to put on her sandals. As she rambled by them, the man tried talking to her. His talk seemed to bug Sandy, and she shook her head at him and did an abrupt about-face. She hurried away as fast as she could.

The man inclined a shoulder up and he tilted sideways. His bony physicality, gangling and loose, radiated a vague malice. He stared in her direction, and over to where she sat. It alarmed Vikki for some reason, and she stood up not knowing why. Maybe it worried her to think he might recognize her if she ran into him later at the waterfront. And then what? She was being paranoid, she said to herself, shaking off the idea. They were weird, though.

About then, a blowsy wind gust lifted her mat and whooshed it around the lawn. And while she rushed to retrieve it, the sun dipped without fanfare into the water. She had missed the sunset by a split second. When she looked at the coast again, the odd man and his companion were nowhere in sight.

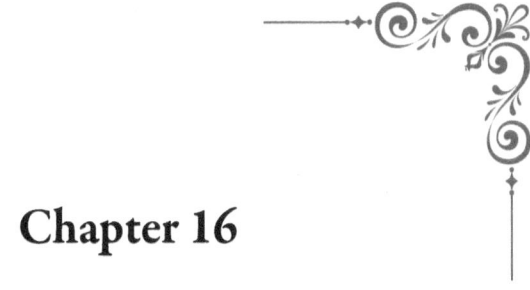

Chapter 16

The black armored Spaar, his official vehicle on state business, was built on the lines of an implacable tank. Two robust cruisers in charge of security led the Spaar while two more followed the file. The heavy machines, buffed to an obsidian luster, rolled on in a slow grind.

Souza waved at the astonished onlookers who had stopped to stare at the convoy. Their expressions changed once they recognized him, going quickly from disbelief to enthusiasm to see him in their neighborhood. Crowds massed about and cheered him on in support.

A man trotted alongside his car. His t-shirt was emblazoned with an image of Souza and the party emblem. He pinched his throat and made a promise to Souza and said he will vote for him come election time. His attentive security blocked the man who shouted his loyalty for the party and Souza despite being pushed back.

At another halt, a wizened grandma in a wheelchair lifted her hands in benevolence. She said she would cast her ballot for him even though her polling booth was miles from her home. Nothing would stop her, she said. Her voice was trembly but resolute, her spirit not one bit frail.

His fans bolstered his spirits. He realized he was in friendly territory now. And that in the midst of a barrage of disapproval, he had genuinely forgotten what approval felt like. For the first time in months he felt a victory was well within his reach. All he had to do was harness that spirit of fidelity and affection and race to the finish line.

But it was going to be a tough slog.

He spotted the signs of a battle ahead already. The farmers' lobby in Goi had aligned with his opponent Carmel Diem and were a hair's breadth away from merging as a group. His emboldened rivals had formed dubious alliances and appeared ready to light a fire under his seat and blast him out of office.

Diem was the flavor of this election year. He licked a finger and held it to the breeze before he took a stand on anything, playing on the electorate's fears. Diem guaranteed the rerouting of Mithula River into Goi's fields in a year if they elected him. Guaranteed! He did not say how. His plan defied logic but became a lifeline to those fed up with the drought. He had scored favorable points for his party with such claptrap.

Besides that, the blowhard seniors in Souza's caucus were more concerned for their seats than his reelection. That did not bother him much; he had tricks up his sleeve to fix them. It was the recent crop of lawmakers who confounded him with their free this and free that hollering. He did not know what to make of the lot. Like seaweed, the novices shifted with the tide. If voters embraced their half-cooked schemes, it was the end of the state as he remembered it.

In private, he admitted his own offensive remained stuck in platitudes. The trite slogans he spouted bored him. And saying the words out loud made him feel sheepish. His campaign missed spark; his speeches ran flat. He wanted inspired thinking, a fresher approach. Novel solutions that gave hope to voters, so they forgot the letdowns of the present. At least until the elections were over. What he urgently needed was a separate set of eyes to look at the issues stalling his campaign.

The convoy slowed and came to a halt for pedestrians and ambling cattle. They let each pass, edging forward until the next passing obstruction. The wide cars were designed to impress and steering them around Nerul's narrow lanes was a challenge. Several tight turns later, they left the town behind. The motorcade continued on to Margosa for his appointment with Mira Tilak whom he had met at a fundraiser years ago.

His closest aides had deserted him like rats leaving a sinking ship; he was not popular at the moment. Their friendship, however, had endured through thick and thin. He did not have to explain things to her because she knew how the system worked.

She came from old money, from a family entrenched in state politics. They were huge Front donors.

When she was twenty-one her shrewd parents arranged her marriage to Nitin Tilak who was from a family equal in standing to theirs. It was a move to secure her future. He was the youngest Front mayor ever elected in the capital. She was educated and good-looking. One could see why the two sides considered it a suitable match.

Soon after the wedding the monsoons arrived and with the weather came doom for the young couple. Rain poured from the skies for weeks, and then for months. Locals said it could be a long monsoon. The sun disappeared under clouds for months at a stretch during a long monsoon, and this was one of those, a season of gray light. It was an accurate forecast, and it rained and rained and never stopped.

As the weather held, the new groom contracted typhoid from the prolonged damp. They rushed him to sunnier climes in hopes he might recover, but he only got sicker. He was gone soon after, on one of the clearest days in the valley's history.

Souza knew she picked up the pieces of her life after the loss and jumped into politics. The then Front governor was running for his second term. She began her career by campaigning relentlessly for his reelection. Her natural talent for grassroots fundraising - and her connections - made her a heavyweight within the party, a genuine rock star. The Governor won the election handily, and she advanced up the ranks and became his principal advisor in record time.

Though she lived on the island, and stayed far from the furor of politics, Souza met with her before every election to exchange notes.

His optimism spiked after their talks and billowed his sails. He hoped today's meeting granted him new breath, honed his wit. Her backing would help him keep the pressure on his opponent till the needle moved in favor of the Front.

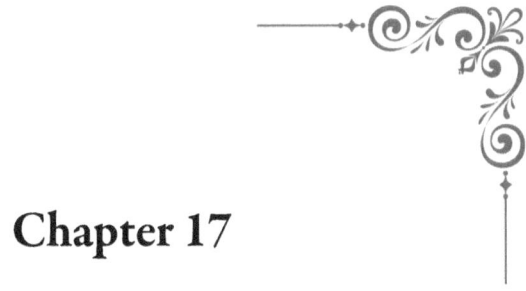

Chapter 17

G reg liked how the sea sprays buffered him from the intensity of the sunlight as he ran. The frequent misting of water on his skin kept things bearable. He tried to time his regular run as the tide receded out to the sea. This was when the smoothened sands had a tricky resistance that he enjoyed. A run completed meant all was well in his world. Or was going to be.

He started at the front gates of Margosa and did a five-mile stretch on the beach. From there he took the main street through the town of Nerul. A back road from the town led to the rear gates at the opposite end of Margosa, and he finished here. The horseshoe-shaped course was a daily routine for him which he rounded off with a yoga session at the studio after.

He slowed his pace as he moved onto lanes with houses built tight together. Painted shutters framed the windows of modest stucco homes, each with a tiny portico and tiled seats on either side. Dozing locals on their porches woke up when they heard him huff and puff. Why anyone dashed about in the noon's heat frying their head was beyond them. The browned children playing on the hot sidewalk were immune to the sun unlike the dozers, and they yelled out a greeting as he went by.

He was near the gates when a sleek black sedan drove by him and coasted through the rear entrance. Four Monitor cruisers tailing the sedan pulled in right after and blocked access. Security dressed in dark uniforms got out of the cruisers.

The gates were situated close to guest cottages inside the resort, and with the sudden closure he would have to go back the route he ran. What a hassle, he thought, coming to a halt at the entrance. He hunched over to catch his breath.

Jass was towing a wheelbarrow with potted plants when the guards spread out and stopped him from taking a further step. He turned around and came up to Greg.

"Gates are closed now. Nobody can enter," he said to him.

"What's happening?" he asked the gardener.

"Big boss man Governor is here today. This means more work for me. Come this way. I know a shortcut."

He grumbled to himself, complaining how this caused too many delays in his schedule. Greg followed him to a gate in a steep wall that wound past the entrance and surrounded the three inland facing sides of the facility. While the gardener fished in his pockets for a key, he watched the guards whose impassive faces stared at nothing. He had no clue who the governor was, but his stoic security officers impressed him.

Chapter 18

G *oi* Souza got the earthquake alert soon after he left the resort, and it reminded him of another cataclysm. One that happened centuries earlier, and during a drought more severe than the current one in Goi. His family had lost a lot of land and property in what was known as the Great Samudri quake.

He watched a live newsfeed of random folk being interviewed at a city bakery. When the persons in line described the jolting, the owner interrupted the interview.

"This is nothing," the owner said. "The Great One was the stuff of legends."

He slapped a crusty loaf onto a scrap of newspaper and taped the ends. And he cast a steely glance around daring anyone to disagree.

The news had no news. Souza called his office, and his aides assured him there was no need to worry. It was business as usual in Goi. The tremor struck a hundred miles below the earth and was too deep to cause any grave damage at ground level. In the capital the land shook a little and some paused and said, 'did you feel that?' But the busy city did not hesitate unless forced to a stop. People moved on with their routines. The earthquake had spared the state, and that was that.

He began thinking about what Mira said to him. She told him the Front had a chance of victory if he remained true to his original platform when he became Governor. And that assessment was on target. Enough with the distractions of news pressers and the meets with influencers. He must rub shoulders with people on the street and draw attention to his many successes. Show them how he met his goals and did what he promised. He felt a weight lift off him.

As they drove to his office in the capital, he got a call from Veliz, the family caretaker in charge of security at the estate. He was a local Finsian who kept fences and managed the occasional tenant skirmish and was good at handling affairs while Souza campaigned. Veliz called only if it was important. And Souza's first thought when he took the call was that Berto had returned to make trouble.

"What is it?" Souza snapped, expecting unpleasant news.

"I saw a strange sight at the south end," Veliz said, a tinge of concern in his voice.

Then he clammed up and refused to elaborate. They talked of other events for a bit, and he hung up the line. The call set him off at a tangent, and he imagined a million matters that could have gone wrong. He leaned forward and ordered the driver to step on the gas. The car flew ahead on the wide four-lane highway with the scenery zipping past them in reverse.

When he arrived at his estate an hour before sunset, Veliz was waiting for him in his truck at the entrance. He dismissed his convoy and got in next to him. The rugged truck bumped on the uneven terrain as they slowly made their approach to the south side.

"This is odd," Veliz said, bringing the truck to a halt. "I went by the well this afternoon and noticed something."

They had come to an age-old step-well, far from the industrial silos which blocked the skyline. The well was in ruins and had not been used for years. He never gave it a moment's thought.

Veliz shone a light at the lowest point, and Souza stretched over the rim for a clearer view of the inside.

"Beam it up," Souza said.

Veliz aimed the light higher at the rock.

"What is that jutting out the wall?" Souza asked.

From where they stood, it appeared to Souza as if the vertical wall had split apart. And instead of a gaping space at the break, a sculpted construction of some kind extended outward. Though he concentrated and followed the beam, the design was beyond his comprehension. Fabricated, perhaps. Or maybe not.

"That's the pinnacle of the old vault city," the caretaker said.

"Enough of that drivel. It is gone. Has been buried for centuries," Souza sputtered. A part of him wanted to believe what Veliz said. And a part of him was exasperated by that want.

"A temblor struck Goi today. I have heard it can push stuff up," Veliz insisted.

Souza's heart leaped. Without saying a word, he climbed down the rough-hewn treads leading to the well's floor. The descent downwards was precipitous. Veliz clutched the stone holds built into the circular walls and scuttered after him.

They halted at the final terrace's edge. The construct soared hundreds of feet above them, the sides thick with algae. Souza rubbed the moss off the exterior, and as he cleared the stone, he uncovered astonishing things. Flying chariots, dancing nymphs and marching warriors were carved in sharp relief on marble, with their features scored into the grain with exactness. Its finial, even in the waning light, gleamed gold.

"I cannot believe it!" Souza said, dazed by the find. He snatched the flashlight from him.

"Look," Veliz said.

He gripped Souza's wrist and directed the light at the water packed with a layer of vegetation. Croaking bullfrogs jumped and slid back into the depths. As they dived in, a myriad round objects floated upwards and got trapped in the leaves.

"What are those?" Souza asked.

Veliz bent frontward, and he plucked at the spherical pieces under the leaves. He straightened up and opened his palm to reveal a glistening coin.

"Pure gold, I am certain," he said.

Souza seized it from him. As he wiped it clean with his shirtsleeve, he saw the familiar bust of a thirteenth century king, the Maharajah of Samudri, engraved on the facade. He angled the beam and swung it at Veliz. The rays shadowed the planes under his bones and the hollows of his eyes.

"I touched nothing," Veliz said, his face tightening.

Souza curled his fingers over the coin.

"Get me more," he said.

Veliz walked down the last flight of steps once again. He reached the bottom, and he drew the thickish water toward him with a stick. The coins drifted closer. He collected what he could and handed them to him.

Souza started the ascent, overpowered by the discovery. As they approached the truck, he turned around and he planted himself before Veliz. His legs rooted to the soil as if he meant to stand there forever. The commands rushed out of him, fast and strong. He wanted to make sure as he spoke that the caretaker's loyalties were unchanged despite the stunning reappearance of the royal vaults.

"Board and fence this place," Souza ordered. "And stay on top with the patrols. Your life depends on it."

Chapter 19

The find controlled every waking second of his life after that, and Souza got sidetracked. He made routine statements at campaign stops and it was clear he was a million miles away from his words. Voters tuned out. The poll numbers reflected their disinterest and sank to a record low for the Front.

His tanking approval sent his critics in the party into convulsions. They lamented he had forgotten his center and would deliver the election on a platter to Diem. Their handwringing compelled him to heed the polls he liked to ignore. Irked by the criticism, he called his deputy for a talk. A perturbed Harris Chacko went over the latest graphs with him. It did not bode well.

Farmers most affected by the drought lived in District 10. The support for him had eroded the most here. And one could see why.

Farmlands in the region that thrived before the drought were now arid wastelands. Withered cattle carcasses, symbols of decay and apathy, littered the landscape. The recent bout of showers brought hope, but water had flowed over the cracked earth and not a drop was absorbed. To add insult to injury, the rain withdrew the next day, traveled westward, and soaked the islands. The islands had plenty of water.

"District 10 has always voted for the Front. They named an entire town after me, dammit," Souza said.

"People are angry, Chief. This drought has dried not just their farms, but their souls. And this is true in all of Goi. Diem has guaranteed them fresh life if he is chosen."

"They will have regret if they choose him," Souza laughed.

"Whether he pulls it off after is not important anymore," Chacko said.

The Mithula River rolled through Carnak first. It then crossed state lines into Goi. Drought had also scorched farms in Carnak. But that state widened a tributary on their side of the river and solved the issue. The down rush of water flooded their farms, violating an older accord signed by both states when flows were bountiful. Souza demanded they shell out the fines for the violations during talks.

And at that point, both sides reached an impasse.

His opponent Carmel Diem was unrestricted by the burdens of office and pesky budgets. He proposed funds for grandiose projects. Like expanding the river at the border. Souza knew low river volumes in Goi made those schemes impossible, but farmers were grasping at straws. They wanted a different fix for the problem plaguing their farms and believed Diem.

"Did the private eye find dirt on him?" he inquired.

His opponent was in the public eye. And Souza thought Diem had lived long enough to have at least one chattering skeleton in his closet.

"Not much," Chacko replied. "Diem wears platform heels to appear taller, the report said. He is vain about his height. Had a mistress or girlfriend in the States back when he was an undergrad. This while his dutiful wife stayed behind in India and cared for the children. I heard he asked her consent, and she gave it."

"What sort asks permission for an affair?" Souza scoffed.

"A tepid scandal by any measure. But things have altered at the present. He now goes home to the same spouse and kids when he is not campaigning. Average student in college, mediocre career. He is the guy of the moment."

"Pfft!"

"That is all we have, Chief," Chacko said, with a resigned shrug.

"Get me something I can use," a terse Souza said when he saw they had wound up empty. "With teeth and claws to it."

They shifted to more pressing issues. He had a series of rallies planned in constituencies that showed robust poll figures in his favor. His speeches centered on the strengths of his party and Diem's inexperience. If he continued in that vein, Chacko thought a win was conceivable come election day.

Just then his secretary interrupted their discussion with a call. When she said a person who refused to reveal his name had news of Berto, he wrapped up the session and dialed the caller on his personal line.

"This is Lala," a man answered.

"The casino king?" a nonplussed Souza asked.

"None other. Your brother Berto owes me a deal of money, Guvnor."

"That is between him and you."

"Pay me what he owes, and we can pretend this never happened."

"Stop dragging me into your bullshit."

"Let us not forget the elections are a dance on a tightrope. Why allow this insignificant matter to become a migraine headache between us, I ask you."

"Take an aspirin for the headache. The answer is no."

Lala then changed from persuasive casino owner to his genuine ruffian nature. Souza let him go on with his bluster and his threats. This was negligible, not the stuff to dent his politicking. But as he hung up, a notion at bay in a corner of his mind moved to the forefront. He summoned Veliz to his ranch.

When the caretaker got there, he assured him he had boarded the old well as instructed. And being a chronic insomniac, he patrolled the property by the hour.

"Never mind that," Souza said to him. "Set up a meeting with Beluga Lala."

Chapter 20

Though Lala objected, Souza insisted that Veliz would be his escort. Lala was more used to giving orders than receiving them.

"I will send one of my guys," he said, miffed.

"No proxies," Souza said.

"Alright. I will come with my bodyguard."

"No bodyguards, and no weapons."

"I go nowhere without my bodyguard. And he goes nowhere without his weapon."

"There is a first time for everything."

"You want to be like me."

"Don't flatter yourself."

"But you are no thug."

"That I am not."

"What is this nonsense about?"

In the end, Lala decided to humor him. He thought this exchange with Souza may be worth his while, despite the aggravation he felt.

Late one night, Veliz brought Lala to the ranch in his truck. Once in his home, they got comfortable in the living room. Food and beverages sat on a coffee table. Souza poured him a drink, and while Lala snacked, he kept up a steady stream of trifling talk with the casino owner. A seasoned Lala understood a thing or two about duplicity. He matched his inanities, talking up a storm of endless trivia in return. The meeting had more to it, and Lala let the evening peel open layer by layer. He roosted in his seat, an image of calm, but was impatient on the inside for Souza to come to the point.

"I am glad we are on the same page on this, Guv. We both know you are in a tight spot with voters. Bad publicity is no good, yes?"

"For me, no. It is not good."

"And no good for Berto, too."

"Berto is a nobody. Why would he care?"

"Souza family name and all."

"If it is Berto you are after, go get him."

"Maybe I will get you, too."

"Stop the saber rattling, fool."

Lala did not know what that meant.

"Speak plainly," he said to Souza.

"Alright, then," Souza said. "You are a joke – with no punchline."

"Tell you what. Pay me what your brother Berto owes - with double interest since he absconded from a debt - and we are even."

"I will do no such thing."

"Why all this then?" Lala said, waving his hand at the spread on the table.

"To wind you up."

"Why?"

"I have a proposition."

Lala's snaggle tooth gleamed when he heard the remark. He drank a pinched sip from his glass and held it together. Souza harbored an important secret. One so threatening he needed the help of a certified gangster like him. He realized he was right.

"Is that so?" he replied in a disinterested way.

"My ancestors built a splendid underground vault system in the 1300s. It disappeared during an earthquake in 1750."

"So what?"

"The recent tremor has brought it to the top again."

"Say what?"

"I have seen the family records. They show clandestine vaults with riches beyond your wildest dreams."

"What?"

The news stupefied Lala. He ditched his act and paced the floor with his arms clutched behind his back and with his head thrust forward in thought. Souza was quiet for a while.

"There's a fly in the ointment, so to speak," he then said.

Lala came to a halt.

"Fly what?" he said.

"If the state finds out, they will take the entire find. That is the current law," Souza said, drawing out his words.

"You got a fix around that?"

"I do. My plan is to work as a team until I figure out a permanent solution. You will receive your share, I promise."

"Give me more details," Lala implored. "Why so stingy?"

Lala was not the analytical kind. As the narrative sank in, he sized his situation. The pieces shifted in his mind and formed an elementary sketch. A child's drawing. He studied the picture from all angles. This was big stuff. Bigger than his smudgy currency laundering casinos, and larger than life itself.

He had guys, a glib Lala said to him. Besides, excavating was a simple job. He knew people who knew people in the business.

They met again in private and continued their talks over the weeks until they struck a tentative deal. But before they sealed the contract Lala demanded proof that the city existed. He insisted on a visit. Souza thought his demand reasonable, and he planned a trip for the following morning.

Neither slept very much that night. Souza stayed up because his distrust of a known crook had him watching for problems already. As for Lala, a motion film in his mind's eye showed him fantastic wealth hidden in secret vaults. In a fever, he imagined himself bathing in gold and dying a fortunate man.

At dawn the next day Veliz led them onward to the site. The three of them began the descent toward the nub of the mystery. Lala wheezed with exertion and excitement and tried to keep pace. His feet were killing him by then, each weighty step was an agony, but he clenched his jaws and bore the pain.

They stopped at the last terrace. Water swished in circles at the perimeter of the well. The sun had slid up the horizon, and the light fell on the marble vaults in a dramatic show. Lala goggled with disbelief. He gripped the stony knob holds, his hands as white as bone.

Frogs in the well croaked in alarm as the rays panned across. The manic hopping of the frogs agitated the flow and lifted objects upwards to the surface. When Souza drew his attention to the gold floating on the thick water, the blood drained from Lala's face. And it gratified Souza to see the balance tip in his favor.

The coins glowed through the murkiness at the water's edge. Lala flopped to the ground on his belly. He reached for them, but his arm fell too short, and he wiggled his fingers in disappointment. Lala looked up in awe at him. Souza leaned to the fore and clasped his wrist in warning.

"Not yet," Souza said. "It happens when I say so."

His wintry grip shocked the flesh, but Lala did not balk. He allowed Souza to pull him to his feet.

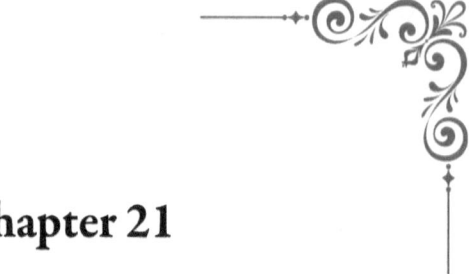

Chapter 21

Sellers at the indoor market piled the produce in reed baskets and sprinkled water across to keep them fresh. The sprinkles alarmed scavenging pigeons which flew to the rafters and preened and fussed up there.

Rego watched his footing near the smushed debris on the ground. He passed the scattering birds and the buyers who critiqued the produce for a lower price. After a quick walk through a busy promenade, he emerged onto a street outdoors.

He had a seat at a food stall and ordered a sugarcane juice. The owner fed canes and gingerroot into a jangling machine that pulverized and juiced them until they turned to straw. He filled a glass at the barrel's faucet and handed Rego the jade green drink.

Rego was waiting for Exit, a two-bit criminal who had spent half his life in prison. He was the department's authorized snitch. A month ago, Exit had walked into police headquarters and offered his services for cash. He was reformed, he said.

Turnover among informants was high. And the police chief took up the offer against his better judgement. The arrangement was not too hot to begin with, and Exit's information had holes nine times out of ten. It finally reached a head, and the chief put his foot down. Snitches on the payroll who did not deliver were out, he said. But Rego would let Exit know that later.

In a while, Exit slinked up to the stall in a traditional ear cleaner's disguise. A cross body bag of tools was strapped across his chest. He held a placard with pictures of the ear debris he could extract for a pittance - wax, stones, hairballs, lost earbud ends and whatnot. It was a look marred by a mock mustache sitting askew on his lip, and about to slide down his chin. Exit was getting sloppy with his getups.

"Fix your whiskers, idiot," Rego whispered.

Exit adjusted the fake fur into place. He was thankful no other customers were there. A snitch had it risky these days.

"I have news of the girl. Her name is Naini," he said. "A pledged girl from Satomi, the town of prostitutes."

"What is a pledged girl?" Rego asked.

"The town pledges girls to a goddess of prostitutes when they become women. All common whores if you ask me."

"Where does she live?"

"Panji."

"What part?"

"She rents digs left of the tracks. But you won't find her there. She disappeared days ago."

"Where to?"

"Her aunt's place on Fins Island. The neighbors said a boyfriend of hers showed after she was gone."

"Who was he?"

"Don't know who he was."

"What did he look like?"

"He had longish hair and a scruffy beard."

"What else?"

"When they told him she had left he went mental. He could be headed to the island too."

"Is she on the island?" Rego asked him.

"Could be," Exit said.

He withheld the details, playing his games. Rego caught the switch in his attitude.

"Heyy!" Rego said, waving a fist at him. "Is she there or not?"

Exit scooted to the distant edge of the bench in a huff. He admitted he had no clue on her whereabouts.

Rego shook off his irritation.

"Any signals from Lala?" he said.

"I heard he called the search off," Exit said.

Rego reached for his wallet.

"You are out. The chief had you fired," Rego said.

Exit grabbed the cash and ran.

Rego updated him on the way to the bus terminal. The man who caused a row fit Berto's sketch. What bothered Kelkar the most though was the news on Lala. Debt collection was his bread and butter. And giving up on an owed loan was contrary to his nature. This latest morsel from their spy nagged at him throughout the drive. Rego complained about everyday politics at the station, but he continued to analyze the lead on Lala. His grumbles slipped past his ears.

Soon they approached the bus terminal, a frenetic hub that connected the mainland to the island. Kelkar closed the ticketing office shutters and the crowd in line buzzed in protest.

The two clerks at the counter had a good look at Berto's picture, and both of them recognized him.

"The guy was smashed when he came up to my window," one of them said. "He bought a one-way ticket to the island."

"I cannot believe he is the governor's brother," the other ticketing clerk said. "He was such a bum."

"He kicked up a ruckus before he left on the last bus."

"Do you recall a light-eyed woman buying a ticket?" he asked the clerks. Neither of them did.

"We work the late-night shift," one said, going back to work at the window. "Day staff may know if she did. They relieve us in an hour."

Though they stayed on for the hour, it proved futile. The day shift workers could not remember anyone who matched Naini's profile.

Chapter 22

Souza was in the thick of his campaign, and in a battle for his political future. His enemies were breathing down his neck, but he had years of practice in the viper nests - the halls of the state. And he fended them off deftly.

Souza started with an interview to a fawning magazine and came out like a rose. He visited an orphanage in a neglected district and did some publicity fluff there. Then he went on to make a generous donation to a nonprofit bio stool bank. He knew full well that the founder of the bank sat on the board of the Goyan Times, a washed-up, insipid rag that said the worst of him.

Souza invited a horde of media types for a press conference right after and praised the excellent work the bank was doing. The Goyan Times came to the event, mentioned the donation in an editorial, and praised the excellent work he was doing.

The photo-ops were a killer. Each one a trump card that boosted his profile and made him look good. And in this way he survived the battle until the next round.

Though his maneuvers had bumped his ranking up in the polls, the slim crowds at rallies around the state troubled him. His numbers dallied well below the counts during his earlier term.

His opponent, on the other hand, struck a chord with unhappy voters. He had inspired them with his messaging. The Alliance party led by a ten percent advantage in recent polls while the Front had fallen behind.

Souza had searched hard for dents in Diem's façade, and he found none so far. It seemed like Diem lived a storybook life. No scandals to speak of, no tawdry shenanigans caught on tape. He was wealthy and photogenic. And his shot at the primaries – the top match in the state - was a punt to the deep end of the pool. The gambit surprised Souza who thought he was a risk averse, plodding sort. Then he watched footage of Diem at a rally and got another view of him.

With a gallery before him, Diem transformed. He drew a spontaneous response from voters. They gifted it to him with no effort on his part.

Souza checked out taped news segments of Diem put together by his campaign. And he had dismissed his cheap rhetoric. He saw those lofty goals of his would not yield any noteworthy results. The state's troubles required a tactical approach and Diem lacked the experience. He had no hard-nosed plan in place. No nitty or gritty to make his vision actually work.

Souza was right on that count, but he had underestimated his opponent's appeal. And unless Diem bungled in a big way, it was not looking great for him. Souza bore the stain of unpopularity. And he was finding it tough to squelch that perception of him in the social media world where these things mattered. The perception that he was an old-world dinosaur whose time had come and gone.

That afternoon, Souza was on his way to address a gathering at a soccer field. Staff had vetted the site and predicted a good turnout of his followers. A formidable speaker himself, he had no need for notes, but he read his talking points all the same. His mind wandered. He was contemplating his speech might go any which way with the audience.

Thirty minutes away from the locale, he looked on either hand of the street and understood there was something wrong with the picture. The throughway was practically devoid of his supporters. He remembered his resounding victory from two years ago. There had been numerous parades held in his honor in the capital after he won the previous election, and hundreds upon hundreds of his smiling fans had packed sidewalks miles ahead of a rally venue.

It was not that long ago. And that one scan of the street made him realize how much his world had changed. The floods had dried to a disheartening trickle.

"More people should be here, Chacko," he said to the deputy governor who traveled with him.

"Our party workers met with local chapters yesterday. They assured us they would come," Chacko said, chewing on his inner cheeks with a frown.

"Spit out the estimates."

"About eight thousand, give or take a few. Party patrons are being bused from other districts. They insisted on being paid if we wanted them to show."

"Well! What a sea change this is," Souza said. He forced a splenetic laugh.

An anxious Chacko glanced at his laptop screen.

"This just in from our media office, Chief," he said. "Diem is addressing a rally close to here. His admirers have camped outside the venue for hours and are willing to pay to hear him speak."

"Sure. Paying to hear garbage."

As they approached the field, a mob of Alliance backers stood with posters that denounced the Front. A smaller group of his allies nearby countered them with praise for him. Though his side stuck to their positions as long as they could, they were outnumbered. The opposite team shut them down with their shouting. At that instant, his phone beeped.

"Rodents are back on the farm. Bait does not work anymore. What should I do?" the text from Veliz said.

In a fit of pique, he lobbed the phone under his seat. He stepped out of the car with expectation. His set smile briefly touched his eyes as he waved to his supporters on the turf. When he grasped that they amounted to less than a hundred, he lost his composure. He was aghast at how low he had slid. A rising sense of despair accompanied his anger, and he turned toward Chacko in fury. He took aim at him, holding him responsible for the debacle.

"This has to be a joke, Chacko," he said, his mouth an ugly gash. "What the hell are you imbeciles in the caucus doing?"

Chacko's shoulders sagged when he saw the sparse audience. The dismal count was a wakeup call, and the signs could not be clearer. His term as deputy and all the attached perks the title came with was likely drawing to an end.

Chapter 23

Few blocks from the soccer field, the Alliance rally was packed. The crowd hurrahed when Diem bounded up the steps and marched toward the podium. His appointees in the front rows gave him a standing ovation. They understood he had breathed life into the party, given them a reprieve. And that his popularity had strengthened their position. As they clapped and cheered him on, they secretly thanked their aligned stars.

Shouts of support picked up steam and became a swell. Diem made a half-hearted attempt at calming the gathering, but he was a politician first and foremost. He gave up and began to revel in their response. The audience roared at his stale quips, and his rehashed wisecracks. Women admirers forgot their better halves next to them, shushed their kids, and watched him spellbound. He basked in the recognition, claimed it as his own.

Diem swore to be their salvation, the hero they had waited for all this time. And he shed copious tears in a show of empathy every chance he got. His followers ate it up. He railed against Souza's policies, and people boomed their approval at him. At each of his rallies, he swore to bring more water to farmland and invest in desalination plants, and this was no different.

Though critics censured him as a single topic candidate, a one trick pony, it was clear that did not matter to voters anymore. The response at the rally was proof. And his popularity had risen along with the grim figures of drought deaths.

At the rally, scores of private security guards stood with their fronts to the crowd. They complemented a team of city police officers who guarded the VIPs on stage. Away from the stage, from one end of the field, Souza supporters yelled slogans against Diem. Tempers flared and opposing groups hurled themselves at each other. The scuffle escalated out of control, and guards abandoned their posts in their rush to the miscreants. And after that, at a section where their presence was the lightest, events reached a frightening point.

Tips Sattu was in place in the audience, and he set in motion the opening part of the plan. The plan put to use a talent Tips had that only Lala and Ludi knew of. Tips was a savvy ventriloquist in his private life, a distinguished fellow at Subvents, a subversive syndicate of voice-throwers. War special effects were his forte.

He began to mimic the audio of a shootout from the gothic serial *Bullet Rain*. His composite voices projected the scenes of a slaughter into the crowd, and chilling cries of agony from bullet ridden bodies could be heard throughout the rally. The sounds were apocalyptic, and so realistic, it had people fleeing from their seats in horror.

On cue, from few rows behind him, Ludi executed the latter part of the plan. He shouted that a bomb had either exploded or might at any second. His warning unleashed a mindless fear that skittered from person to person, as it was meant to do.

Diem's speech drowned in the screams. He lost significance with the panicked crowds and was soon talking to an audience of none.

City police called in reinforcements, flew in a bomb squad, blocked streets and traffic and evacuated everybody. In other words, they had a big mess to clean.

This happened at other Diem rallies where exchanges between the bad actors and spectators stopped his speeches. And innocents trapped in the melee dispersed and fled the venue. The Alliance blamed Souza for the riots, but when he interviewed on talk shows he skimmed over the issue and insisted his hands were clean. His anemic replies failed to satisfy his opponents who took to the streets in protest.

Days later, when matters calmed, Lala and Souza met at his ranch. The casino owner told him he had contracted with his associate Max Sing for a delivery of trucks. He made up a story, he said, of plans for a casino franchise out in the country. It was very hush-hush, he assured Souza. His own trusted men ran the operation, and he would deal with any setbacks if and when they arose.

"Did you hear about the fights at Diem's rallies?" Lala said to him with a chortle.

"Who knows if that stuff works," Souza said, ducking the question.

He treaded shady waters with Lala, a lifelong criminal. The snares lay deep. And although willing to play along in the beginning, he now saw the reins slip and float away from him.

"You fret too much, G. All is well," Lala said with that laugh again.

He played down Souza's doubts and tossed a peanut into his mouth.

Though carefree on the outside, Lala weighed him on his internal scales. This was typical of Lala who probed happenings in his own simple-minded manner. Then, at a ripe moment, he would turn the knife in the cut until he had the advantage.

Chapter 24

ins Island

F Greg felt as free as a bird in an airstream as each foot dropped after the next. The run became a moving meditation. Though he preferred his own company, he did not mind that Vikki had tagged along with him. They got on well.

A sprinter in her college years, she pushed off at a steady clip and had scooted ahead of him onto the main street. As she ran by the street, glints from a slapdash stall on the wayside shot across her eyes. She waved at the desert nomads selling the mirrored skirts. An eager seller rushed forward, and the others joined him. They milled around her and displayed the merchandise for a look-see. She would bring them luck if she bought something, they said. Anything.

Meanwhile, he zipped past Vikki and the colorful group into town. He slowed as usual once he hit the narrow lanes where residents dozed on their stoops. His puffing in the midday heat did not seem to bother them anymore. They made mild disapproving sounds as he passed and then continued with their siesta.

When tires screeched further up the lane, it brought him to a stop. The nappers woke up. They stared at the black Spaar with tinted windows rounding the curve. The car raced inches past him and nearly slammed into a flock of sheep emerging from a courtyard. He flattened his frame against the walls of a house right in time and escaped a hit. Behind him, he saw Vikki plastered to the wall as he was. The car disappeared around the next bend.

"Can you believe that maniac driver?" she said. "He just about knocked us over. I got a pic of his license plates in case he ends up killing somebody later."

He walked up to her.

"The same car was at the retreat days ago. Jass said it belonged to a political bigwig from Goi," he remarked.

She zoomed in on the image on the rear plate.

"It is a state car, for sure. Look at those plates with the insignia," she said, swiping at the screen.

The herder calmed his flock. He touched the animals with his crook and steered them in the correct direction. When a frisky lamb jumped at her and pleaded to be picked up, she scooped it into her arms. She cooed into its ear for a minute, then handed the woolly baby to the herder with a sympathetic nod.

"This road was not created for speed. It is a wonder the moron did not kill these adorable little creatures," she said.

Chapter 25

Traffic had slowed to a protracted stop on the bridge. Motorists in a hurry honked horns, and they yelled out of windows into space, angry at a situation beyond control. Sounds jumped from one car to the other and fused into a cacophony. The span lacked emergency routes, and so when matters went wrong, everything ground to a halt. People let loose and it got crazy.

Condé Jarillo Rodrigo Fonseca de Crossingro, a seafaring aristocrat, commissioned the twenty-mile-long sea bridge in 1698. He had arrived on the island with a fleet of trading caravels some two hundred years after Vasco da Gama touched land. The bridge connected Fins to Goi and had no name as such, but as time passed locals called it the Crossing.

The traffic channel on the radio reported on an accident further on, and drivers were advised to proceed with caution as they progressed up the bridge. Kelkar lowered the sound and settled back. A wait lay ahead.

"How do you know the Governor, sir?" Rego asked.

He had grown up with five siblings in a home full of chatter. Drawn-out silences made him uncomfortable, and it was obvious he wanted to talk.

"It is a lengthy story," Kelkar said.

"If you don't mind, I'd like to hear it," Rego said with plain eagerness.

Kelkar smiled, and he put his notepad and pen away.

"Many years ago, I investigated a brutal murder in Goi," he began. "One evening, we found a wealthy couple tortured and robbed. Their teenage granddaughter was beaten to death. It happened around the time my wife died, and I threw myself into the case."

"We got a break after weeks of dogged work. It led us to a neighbor who lived right next door to the murdered girl. In fact, he was the one that contacted police to report suspicious activity at the house. He had wailed and howled the loudest when officers showed."

Traffic pitched forward and stopped. They inched across the steel decks which blazed white hot under the sunlight. At the other end of the span was Fins Island. The characteristic, red-tiled roofs of island houses leapt from the dark green cover of trees.

Below them, a tugboat chugged along with a queue of log rafts. Fishing schooners sped by foaming the waters. And swooping pelicans dived beak first into the surf and reemerged with a catch.

The sea was a limitless bowl of molten ultramarine.

"The same neighbor's teenage son killed the young woman because she broke off their relationship," he continued. "And the boy's father helped. He hired the killers who terrorized the grandparents while the son slipped upstairs and brutalized her. I carted the man and the boy to the police station. In a moment of weakness, I slapped the pair a tad. When the suspects' family learned about it, they yelped for a lawyer. They hired none other than Oni Palani."

"I am sure phony Oni loved being the center of attention," Rego said with a laugh.

Palani was a showman, a publicity hound who took on any case that brought him fame. Some media outlets with nothing to do on slow days covered his antics.

"You bet. His mug shot splattered the front pages," he went on. "He proclaimed his clients were innocent victims of police brutality. Though it was far from the truth, they demanded my resignation and did a big song and dance about the incident. When sources found out the father worked for the opposition it got worse. The affair mutated to a farce, a show of theatrics by the two parties. They lobbed the ball of corruption at each other."

"Politicians. They are scum," Rego said, shaking his head.

"Scum de la scum. Anyway, to keep it short, my career was heading for disaster. At the police chief's urging, I contacted Peter Souza. We met at his office and hit it off. He was an influential party treasurer for the Front, and he used his influence to transfer me to a different branch for a period. As the dust settled, I got the old job back and carried on in the force. He was elected Governor in a rout years later."

At the distant point of the bridge, a tow truck with blinking lights made arduous progress. Cars moved through a gap and quit the jam. He raised the radio's volume. When the station reported two left lanes were free, Rego shifted in that direction.

They picked up speed and exited at Bolim.

"Any good eateries here, Rego?" he asked, changing the subject.

He realized he had not eaten a bite since that morning.

"Temperado, at the street's intersection. Worth a drive. Rain or shine," Rego said, looking upbeat.

Kelkar watched with skepticism as they drove past a gloomy animal shelter. Stir-crazy animals filled the wire cages. Then by a seedy hookah bar. Going out of business ads were on the next block of forlorn stores. A beat-up gym with open doors was at the top of the block. In a sandpit inside, oiled wrestlers in loincloths struggled to gain a grip on each other, and a pair of strutting jungle fowl dodged flying limbs and rolled in the pit. The birds ruled the mud, fluffing themselves and seeming bigger than they were.

They arrived at Temperado to a full house, but the owner gave them priority and escorted them to a table. The interior surprised him. Real palms at the foyer lent the restaurant an oasis-like charm. And somewhere in the background, water from a fountain splashed into a mosaic pond. Light flooded through a round skylight and spotlighted a lady playing folk songs on a piano. Quite nice, he thought.

They decided on 'Fins assado caril leitao,' the restaurant's specialty, and a famous Portuguese dish which first appeared on the menu in the 1700s. The dish was still cooked the same way on Fins Island.

A new pig marinated for twenty-four hours in port wine, saffron, vinegar, peppercorns and its own juices. The next evening, the steeped pig was roasted over coals and served with a rich sauce prepared from the drippings.

The food came to their table and Kelkar had a taste. He nodded his appreciation at the smiling bearer who folded up the tray table and left them to enjoy the meal.

"Leave for Goi tomorrow while I check leads on the island. Get on Lala," he said to Rego.

"What did you have in mind, sir?" he asked him.

"Tail him, make inquiries, and report to me."

"But he is no longer chasing Berto."

"Did you ask yourself why?"

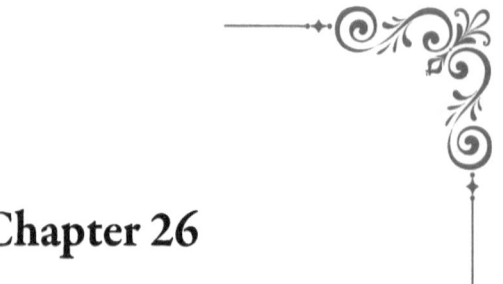

Chapter 26

Berto was trapped in a bad dream, and he flailed his arms while he slept. A spectral swarm was chasing him through a mysterious forest in the nightmare. Shapeless figures snatched at the bag in his arms with hooked talons, and their panting outbreath covered his skin with spittle. The bodies faded when he pummeled them, only to reappear behind him stronger than ever. Before he could outrun them, an apparition twisted his shirt into a knot, waking him up.

He whimpered with relief and opened his eyes to the sunrise. His woken state had all the makings of the same awful dream. He undid the knot in his shirt and tried to think of a way out. If he were to survive, he knew he must.

"I think I can, I know I can," he sang out loud to spur himself on.

But it was of no use. Everything was as clear as grubby bathwater. A weeklong hangover had sapped his energy, wrung him dry. And all the thinking and singing to keep his spirits up had tired him out. He ended the struggle, and as soon as he stopped, a thought broke loose of the muck and floated upwards. The image of his buried stash danced in front of his eyes and comforted him.

He had bought the charas from a mute barber named Firki who plied a covert dope trade, a side business. This was days before he left for the island. When he hesitated to buy, the barber was hurt. He jabbered at Berto with his hands. Would I lie to my best customer, he appeared to ask him. He crossed his heart and bragged that his stock was from the pristine Himalayan foothills. The best of the best, he insisted. Though he doubted Firki, a known fibber, he negotiated with him anyhow and purchased his product.

At the grove, he dug out the sandy clay from under a coconut palm tree with a corkscrew trunk. His nails chipped with the effort, but he kept at it until he retrieved a canvas bag from the hollow. The bag contained petite packets of charas, each weighing about one tola or half an ounce. If all went to plan and if the barber's word in fact proved true, it would sell fast on the island. Dopeheads were a dime a dozen here, and quality stock like his did well in beach towns.

What he had to watch out for were the island's dealers. They ran slick operations, and on a grander scale than a dabbler like him. Vicious dealers on their home turf were the biggest danger, and it was game over if they came across a stray dealing in the open.

The bay winds were still far out at sea. And at noon the sun held at its apex, in its brute state. He searched for shelter, for a cool shady place to nap, but he had walked far from the grove. There was nothing other than exposed beach around him. Berto knew this was an ideal tanning spot for tourists and so he pushed on, dragging his feet along the sands.

He almost gave up when he came to a lane that snaked from the beach into town. But then a man in a flowery shirt that screamed tourist sauntered in from the lane. He blinked at the man, gauged him. The guy's jumpy manner was a dead giveaway, and Berto perked up at the prospect of a sale. He was sure this was going to be an easy score.

"Fine weather today! Can be nicer with some *malai*, some cream on top, no?" Berto said, creeping nearer to the man.

The encounter unnerved the tourist, and he slid away from Berto. He flicked his joint on the sands and mashed it with his flip-flops.

"You a cop?" the tourist asked him.

"No, no, not at all. I hate all cops," Berto wheedled. He affected a laugh and tilted sideways at him as if he were a friend. "I have superior quality, all-natural mountain charas. It is primary grade, not cheap junk from the valleys."

And in a few quick seconds the deal was done. The cash in his pockets charged him with such an instantaneous rush, he began to count it at once.

"Hey! You new here?" somebody said.

The disembodied voice had come out of nowhere and it confused Berto. Then the gangling man materialized before him. His woman companion stood a few steps away.

"What's it to you?" he said to the man.

"You unloading stuff here on Bolim?" the gangler said.

There was a roughness to the skeletal stranger and the question crackled in the gap between them.

Berto squared his jaw to look tough, and he dusted sand off his pants with a nonchalance he did not feel. He tried hard to subdue the wave of panic racing through him. Should he call for help? And from whom? He did not know a soul here.

"What stuff?" he said.

When he heard his words spill out in that shaky fashion, Berto recognized he was in serious trouble. He retracted his head, but the gangler offered him no quarter. Mere inches separated them.

"Charas, ganja, gurda, hash, skunk, weed - that type of stuff. This beach belongs to Tinnu Chacha. You do not dump here unless you want to die."

The man grabbed at Berto's neck with bony fingers.

"What's in your bag?" he demanded, pulling at the bag with his unencumbered arm.

On the verge of blackout, Berto gave up resistance, convinced he was really going to die. It was the woman who saved his life. She shouted out, and caught unawares by her protest, the gangler let go of him. Berto staggered backwards. The man now directed his rage toward the woman, his fist drawn back. He prepared to strike her, then changed his mind and swung his attention to him again. Before the pair left, the man aimed a kick to his temple and knocked Berto's lights out.

Sometime later Berto stirred awake. The last memory he had was the sharp impact of a kick to his head. After wandering in circles for some time, he came to the retaining wall that bordered Margosa. He sat on the capped top of the wall for a rest.

Berto studied the slim woman clearing grass clippings on a pathway ahead absentmindedly for a while. The side-to-side swishing of her broom grew noisier as she made her way toward him. She shifted even closer. He stared at her slender nape, the movement of her limbs, and realized she was Naini. The nametag pinned to her uniform showed she worked at this place.

When he stood to call out to her he saw security patrol on the far side of the pathway, and he sat down quickly and crouched low. Seeing the guards dashed icy water on the hope surging up in him. He knew he stuck out, and so he hurried away before they spotted him.

The wall curved higher from the beach following the lay of the land and became overgrown with thorny creepers. He trailed by the wall for miles until he came to a pair of open gates. Past the entrance, a walkway with thick landscaping led to a front office and to the woodlands beyond. He slipped by the gates and went into the brush and hid.

Evening came, and when she did not appear, he started to leave. It surprised him then to see her glide down the path with a broom and a wicker basket at her hip. Her clothing rustled as she strolled by. Her neat hair combed tight was different and unlike what he remembered. If he lunged out to touch her, she might jump.

He waited until it was dark, biding his time, and then he scuttled up to the work shed where she spent the nights. Though he groped at the door handle and jiggled it, the flimsy lock maintained a firm strength.

The handle's clicking woke Naini up. Her eyes widened and adjusted to the dark. She could barely see inside the room, and so she listened carefully to the creak of the handle's turn. The sawing clack and scrape of the bolt sounded like someone was forcing the door.

She drew the curtain aside from a grilled window to let the light in. The feeble light from a streetlamp fell on sundry tools and objects on the wall shelves. When she reached for a garden shovel on the wobbly shelf, an empty pack of crates clanked to the floor. She ducked and treaded between the fallen stack and wedged the shovel's grip under the knob to secure the door.

On the other side of the door Berto heard tools fall and make a racket. The noise alarmed him and had him faltering backwards. Some other day she would run out of her luck, he said to himself in anger. He loped to the next building, a ramshackle conservatory with potting supplies, staying deep within its shadows. In the dimness, he examined the angles of the door. Once he discovered that a simple latch locked the slatted entrance, he jerked the ends of the clasp and wrenched the bolt from its screws.

Bags full of wood mulch, compost and yard soil lay against the inner walls. Starter saplings in terracotta pots crowded the shelves. He shook the dust and bugs off a rumpled jute bag that was on the floor. Then he spread the bag out and sank down on it and was asleep as soon as he closed his eyes.

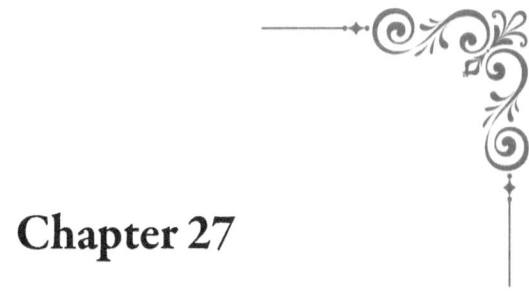

Chapter 27

The bad bird croaked on its journey to the sea and the plaintive cry sent a shiver up her spine. When she was little her mother had said hearing the bad bird's croak brought terrible news to the listener. She told Naini to shut her ears. It does not, Naini had scoffed. And she had laughed at the severe expression marking her mother's face thinking it was funny.

She thought of that and sat up, and she wrapped her arms over her knees and watched the door all night.

When the sun rose, she felt calm despite the night's events, and she prepared for the day ahead. She changed into her work clothes, pinned her tag on the fabric. Then she slid a hairpin over a calendula flower and attached it to her braid.

Her reflection in the fogged mirror gazed back at her. A slanting sunray struck the glass just so, reminding her of that morning, of the exact hour before she was pledged to Daro. The women wove a flower garland into her plaited hair, tugging firmly downward at the parted sections. And before the rituals got underway her mother skated her finger on her kohl-lined eyelid and then dotted Naini's dusky cheek with the blackened fingertip. To ward off the evil eye, she had said.

Naini took a kohl pencil from her bag. She sharpened the tip and pressed it at her chin's dimple to form a black dot, to console herself.

Out in the garden the red flowers on flame trees sailed high, grazing the blue skies. Sunshine flowed over the earth, and the light enveloped her and colored her with gold as she stood there by the window.

Late in the afternoon she arrived at the house and began her chores, humming a tune as she worked. The bells on her anklets chimed as she swept the leaves on the veranda into a heap. At the patio, she wiped under a chair with the broom, and it astonished her when she found Rish seated there. She stopped mid-tune and smiled at him; her lids lowered partway over her glittering eyes.

Chapter 28

It was morning again, and she went outdoors and washed the sleep from her eyes with a splash of water from the faucet. A bracing wind eddied and looped, and the air was sharp and fresh. The sun's light dappled between the trees and traipsed across the flower bushes like a traveling blessing.

She stepped on the cool dewdrops sparkling on the grass tips. Through the quiet came the usual working sounds of other employees going on with their tasks. She drew comfort from hearing the snap of a pruned branch, the rhythm of a rotating sprinkler nearby. And from far, the tart exchanges among the gardeners unwilling to do more than necessary for their jobs.

Then the press of a hand dug so deep into her arm she stopped and gasped. She hurtled over and her things slipped from her. When she turned to see who it was, she saw Berto there. The lurking door rattling specter had returned. He locked on her wrist, but she twisted free from his clasp and backed off from him.

"You! What are you doing here?" she snarled, moving further away.

"I am in a mess. Lala's men will kill me if I do not return the money," he said.

He was in want of her sympathy, her pity even, but she would have none of it.

"Ask your big shot brother for help. Like you always do," she spat at him.

"Let's run away together," he said.

"Get lost," she said.

Her taunts pierced him to the quick. She was the same old scorn dispensing Naini. Stung, he sprang up to his feet. She stormed right back at him, and he came crashing down on the bare spines of a bush. The thorns tore his shirt and ripped his skin.

She grabbed her supplies and basket and ran before he attacked again. A frisson of fear rippled inside her as she relived what had happened. She saw Selvam walking toward her and she cut short her running and erased any trace of concern written on her face. It was not his business anyway, she thought. She looked the other way until he went past.

Up ahead, Jass was dragging a compost sack over the flowerbeds.

"There is a strange man near the supply shed," she said, alerting him.

Jass dumped the sack, and he stripped his gloves off, welcoming the diversion from his gardening duties. She pointed at the spot where she had pushed Berto to the ground. Meanwhile, his assistants grouped closer and marched out in that direction. They came back a short while later, joking about an imaginary intruder and shaking their heads at her.

"There is nobody there. You scared him off, Naini," Jass said, putting on his gloves.

"I must have," she retorted with a derisive laugh. She collected her belongings.

At the house, she swept the tiles from corner to corner until they shone. When she finished, she leaned at the wall and wiped the dust off her clothing. He walked over and gathered her close in an embrace.

"What is the matter today?" Rish whispered into her hair.

His hands spanned the sides of her waist, the small of her back. She closed her eyes and sighed.

"It is nothing," she said, her voice hoarse in her throat.

Chapter 29

The next day staff found the conservatory doors open, with the metal bolt that held them together broken in pieces. Footprints from the outside stopped at a crumpled jute sack spread on the dirt floor in the interior. The plummy odor of alcohol lagged in the air, and there were obvious signs somebody had used the room at night.

Jass sent his assistant to the front office to let Tara know about the happenings. The break-in alarmed her, and she called a locksmith and changed the locks by the day's end. A carpenter she hired for a shelving job at the office agreed to put the ongoing project on pause. He fixed the damaged door, fortified the slats and replaced the worn hinges. His workers swapped the dim lights for brighter ones.

She trusted her staff, took them at their word. They were all locals who worked hard and went to their homes at night. Everyone except Naini. She decided she must have a closer eye on her from now onwards.

When Selvam got home later in the evening, she told him what happened.

"Someone crashed the conservatory," she said, shaking her head in disbelief.

"I cannot imagine why," Selvam said.

"Exactly. We store only mud and seeds in the room."

"Is the new employee put up there?"

"Naini is at the smaller work shed across from it."

"Jass said she was attacked."

"That's news to me. By whom?"

"A stranger. The thing is, when I saw her that day, she had a certain look. Like she knew the person who did."

"Hmm."

"A woman of mystery."

"She is capable. And attractive, don't you think?"

"Have not noticed."

"Liar."

He smiled at her, and she stretched out beside him.

"I wonder if her attacker is the same individual who broke in. It is a bizarre coincidence," she said.

"Remember the time when Jass forgot to lock the doors one night?"

"And a bunch of goats came by in the morning."

"Check if he locks up after hours."

"Good idea."

Jass had wasted a full afternoon rounding up the spirited goats on that day. She was sure he learned from the episode, but maybe he needed a reminder. Besides that, there were no security breaches ever at Margosa. That anyone might steal in did not cross her mind at all.

"I should bring up the matter with Ronnie this coming week," she said.

Ronnie Barbosa, the public affairs manager, met with staff each month to compile their reports and assign budgets. He was a genial sort but ran a tight ship. Tara felt she ought to brief him.

Selvam disagreed.

"Hold off for the present. Maybe the intruder sheltered overnight and is gone from the area," he said. Tara hoped he was right.

Chapter 30

Berto scaled the gate rails and went over to the inside. The jump to the ground jarred his bones, and he picked himself up with a moan and made his way to the conservatory to spend the night there.

When he reached the building, he noticed right away it looked different. The doors did not budge try as he might to push them. Overhead lights cast a bright beam around, and the rays fanned out to the work shed where Naini was. He drew back, afraid of being seen.

He had no place for the night, nowhere to go. There was a vacant spot in the shrubbery that seemed good to lay down and sleep on and he wriggled in. The springy ferns smoothed into a soft bed with the weight of his body, and he curled sideways on an elbow and slept with his ear to the earth. It stayed quiet for a while, and then the crickets made themselves heard. The crisp ripping of their raptor legs on grass sounded loud and too close for comfort, and he could imagine all kinds of arachnids with pincers scurrying in the darkness and crawling on him. Creeped out by the bugs, he stood up and slunk off seaward.

Tonight, just as when he first landed on the island, a bonfire burned by the incoming breakers. The gangler and his woman companion sat by the crackling flames. Berto retreated behind the trees and watched the couple and saw that he had caught them in the middle of an argument.

The man loomed above her, and she shrank from him and slumped backward. His corrosive voice reminded Berto of the day he jumped him, and he felt his chest tighten with apprehension. He slipped further into the trees and continued to watch them argue with each other. In a turn, the gangler leaned closer, and she scissored her arms over her head in defense. He wrapped his hands across her throat, and she thrashed about and gripped his wrists to loosen his hold. In moments, weakened from the effort, her limbs slid from her and fell to the ground. Berto was certain she was dead, and the gangler lying prone on her limp body seemed as if he was dead too.

An errant wave surged on top of them, trapping the man its drift, and he gasped as water flooded his mouth. He groped at the flowing sand till he recovered his footing, and he ran to the east and away from the scene. His elbows pumped hard as he ran, and he kept running until he disappeared out of sight.

Surf rocked the motionless woman, lifting her and then setting her down with a fluid gentleness. The stronger rip currents soon took charge and pulled her from the sandy rim, slow and sure.

By and by a full moon rose and bathed the seashore with its milky light. Berto was still frozen in his space with his sights set on the body near the bonfire. A time later, he emerged from the trees. His fear of the gangler had him terrified at first, and he looped around like an animal driven mad by an itch beyond reach. It was a while before he comprehended the coast was desolate for miles in every direction and coming out into the open he stopped at the flames that split and snapped.

He fished inside their backpack and found rolls of cash tied with elastic bands. Thrown in with the cash were zipped bags of dope but he knew those would be too dicey to sell. He ignored the dope and hurriedly put the rolls into his pockets, and then he shoved some of the loose cash laying at the bottom into his shirt front. He clutched at the lumps of money, laughing at what he had discovered.

Berto fled westward to the refuge of the waterfront restaurants, and he inched along in their shade for cover. He was short of breath and ready to crash, but cursed sleep never came. The night granted Berto a respite, and only until the gangler resumed the hunt for his stolen goods in the morning.

Meanwhile, the gangler had returned to the scene at the beach. He walked to a sandbank and rummaged through the backpack washed up on its mound. When he realized the money was missing, he grew frantic, and he stared at the ocean for someone to blame, but the swells had carried his lifeless partner into deeper, more treacherous waters.

Chapter 31

When he noticed Tara approach, Jass cleared his tools. He stacked them in the wagon and wheeled it off the path. She mostly left him alone while he puttered around with his gardening duties, and it made him wonder why she was there today. He snuck a careful look over the yard and gave it a once-over. It seemed fine. The mowed grass and the landscape in full bloom appeared pruned and tidy, and the pathways were free of clippings and waste.

"How are things here?" Tara asked, motioning to him.

"Okay," he said.

"I heard Naini complained about an intruder."

"She did. Somebody bears her a grudge, I think."

"Did she say what happened?"

He nodded, relieved the matter concerned Naini and not him.

"She said a man attacked her. We checked it out but found nobody. Later though, I saw empty beer bottles where she spotted him. Paper receipts, trash, and... other stuff."

"You must report issues like these to me at once. We cannot have our guests here under any threat."

"Okay."

"Do you lock up the gates in the evenings?"

"Yes, every day."

"What makes you suspect she is in trouble?" she said, softening her tone to put him at ease.

"She is on the run, is my thinking," he replied.

His account of the incident worried Tara, and she started to believe this situation with the intruder might be graver than she first thought. Maybe problems followed Naini. Or maybe she had brought them upon herself. Either way, it became clear she must update Ronnie on the incident at the staff's coming monthly meeting.

Chapter 32

P. Jha toddled over when he saw her at the front office.
"What is it I can be doing for you?" he said, bustling forward. His stained mouth opened wide in an amiable smile.

"Is all this stuff made on the island?" Vikki asked him, pointing to the gorgeous stone pottery on a shelf.

He reached for a dish, and he pointed at the inked word 'Kori' on the underside. The tribe were the early inhabitants of the island, he said.

"They are the most original tribal group of hereabouts," Jha said. "They have a whole superb crafts festival this week at beach. Lots of tourists like yourself are dropping by with willingness for their observing."

"How do I get there?"

"You can walk by the coast lining, and it is bang facing your person. Cannot miss sight. But too late to go now. I am meaning to say, for you is totally not safe to go. Morning is better, then batches of peoples are about."

She walked onto the beach. Her hair waved and drifted with the wind as she increased her pace, and it matched how she felt inside. Despite his caution, hustling locals did not concern her. People packed the cozy restaurants and bars along the seawall, and she liked the phantasmagoric verve of the evenings when the island came alive with humanity. Peppy music, bright lights, and the delicious food lent her spirit an added boost.

Further on, she halted at a crush of laughing tourists swaying to a synthesizer's thumps. She eased between the group. Before she knew it, a jolly man dressed like a Santa on an island vacation gripped her hand and twirled her about. His eyes closed with merriment, and she smiled and indulged him for a bit, pairing her steps with his. The mass parted and the incoherent man let go. He tottered and melted into the throng.

The press of bodies drew her in further. When she tried pushing through, the crowd jostled her and swept her onto a narrow-arched bridge. The height allowed her an advantage, and she saw a lawn party happening on a mansion's spacious grounds from the top. Below, fat koi swam in mesmerizing spirals in a pond. In front of her, a meadow of wildflowers rolled from edge to edge.

On the meadow, cabanas with airy drapes had tables with elegant arrangements and wide platters of food. Outside the tents people sat and passed chillums around, and a musky, vaporous smoke layer hung over their heads. She realized she had mistaken a beach party for the festival, and she shifted from the group for air.

Crowds thinned as she carried on, and she squeezed through the spaces until she came to a meandering walkway. The path curved ahead of her and disappeared into a coppice of trees. Above the treetops, sea gulls called and swooped in drifting orbits in a sunshiny sky. She took the trail with the birds in her sights, guessing the ocean lay in that same direction.

As she continued past the bend, a hatchet-faced man was standing in the way, blocking her path. A thin man with his hair in dreadlocks was scrooched at one side of the path in a rhododendron thicket. The knobs of his bony spine rippled under his skin. She froze when she made out his battered face. It was the odd man who cruised on Bolim beach. A third man with glinting metal teeth stood by the thin one. She heard yells, and the thuds of blows pounding flesh and bone. Vikki glanced away; the less she saw the better. They had some funny business going on.

"Party's the other way, miss," the hatchet-faced man said.

He spoke with an accent she could not place.

"I was on my way to the festival but got lost," she blurted.

"Go back and turn left at the fork," he said.

His cagey face showed he did not believe her. And he waited, his eyes on her, until she withdrew with haste.

She parked herself on the sands once she was on the beach, glad that she was far from the crowds and had her breathing space. While she was thinking what to do next, a boat pulled into shore. Boatmen dumped their catch of netted fish from the deck into the sea, and the crew crooned as they towed the teeming nets inland.

"My boat is the Lord," the lead said.

"Lord of the seas," said the chorus.

My boat is the Lord,
Lord of the seas.
My boat is the Lord,
Lord of the seas.

They unloaded their nets of flopping fish, joshing each other as they worked. When she asked them for directions, they signaled to rows of flapping pennants in the distance.

"Over there!" they all said.

She got to the festival's entrance, and she paused by a crowd to watch costumed Kori women dancing round a lone drummer at the center. He drummed out a hypnotic tempo, his head sliding up and down to his own beat. The singing Kori formed a circle by the drummer, their silky treble voices lending a sense of urgency to the dance.

The performance ended, and the dancers and singers took a break. She moved on over to the rows of handicraft stalls to see what they had. Maybe she would find an art piece like the ones showcased at the office. A thing that slipped into her suitcase with ease. Or a special souvenir or framed miniature. One that was extraordinary, but harmless enough to pass by airport customs with no bothers.

She did find a thing she liked at one stand. It was a droll black onyx box mounted with a snake's skull, with its pointy fangs narrowed to sharp ends. She held the hinged box in her hands and the feel was as slick as chilled butter to the touch. An elderly woman at the shop flashed her a toothless grin and went on with her knitting.

"Only $100," she said, unraveling her yarn ball, but with her foxy little eyes on Vikki.

Vikki thought it was too pricey. The woman sensed her indecision, and she rose from her seat and plucked other objects from a wicker bin to keep her engaged. Out flew crude paintings etched with what appeared to be blood. It was hard to know if it was human or animal blood, and though interested, Vikki did not ask. She held up shrunken baby antelope heads tied together next and brandished them like a toy rattle. Then she tossed the heads back into the bin. Oh, no, Vikki said to herself. What other horrors were in there? She thought to leave but she was charmed by the snake skull box and wanted to buy it. As she got ready to bargain for the item, something else grabbed her eye and she put the box down on the counter.

A feathered headdress lay at the bottom of the bin, the plumes changing color with the tiniest puff of air. She pointed at it and the tribal reached in and gave it to her. They haggled for a while and set the price. She paid for the souvenir and then she wandered about the displays, absorbed by the spectacle around her.

The sun had dipped to the horizon. Shadows lengthened and the stalls lit up. Her legs ached from all the walking, and she made her way back to Margosa before the light waned any further.

At the front porch, Sandy lounged at a table set with a pitcher of cold Darjeeling tea. She joined her at the table and stretched for a glass.

"Been out shopping, have you?" said Sandy who had seen her bag.

She poured her some iced tea.

"Thanks. Yeah, I dropped by the Kori festival. There is a fabulous crafts exhibition going on," Vikki said, placing the frosted glass against her warm forehead to cool off.

"Buy anything interesting?"

Vikki took the headdress out from her bag and gave it to her. Sandy examined the circlet of feathers.

"These are from the raiding Fan-tailed Cimmerian," Sandy said.

"What are they?" Vikki asked.

"A class of magpie indigenous to the island. The birds are a rarity these days."

"I thought of my Grandma Daisy when I bought that," Vikki said with a chuckle. "She owned an ostrich farm and a shop in California which sold everything ostrich. Ostrich fans, ostrich boas and other ostrich what-have-yous. She even had a pet ostrich named Dilley who painted."

Sandy laughed.

"I am serious. She soaked his feet in vegetable dyes, and the crazy bird created artwork as he ran across a blank canvas!"

"Did she sell any?"

"A ton. Customers loved his stuff. They sold out every time."

"Does she still have the farm?" Sandy asked, amused by the story.

Vikki shook her head.

"One day Dilley was being temperamental. She was legally blind by then and she did not see his kick coming. The blow landed square on her, and she died on the spot."

"Poor thing."

"Never trust an ostrich."

"A bird with eyes bigger than its brain," Sandy remarked.

An eagle owl's resonant call cut through their laughter. Sandy gazed skywards. She studied the fuzzy shape of the night hunter, its ear tufts stark white against a blackening sky. The bird soared higher until the voracious darkness swallowed it whole.

Chapter 33

A nervy Sandy, perched at her chair's edge, seemed ready to bolt. The herbalist at the spa prepared the oils, and the unfamiliar scents swirled in the room, overwhelming her. Lavender and rose mingled with spicy myrrh and frankincense, and the vapors swept up her nostrils until she thought she might swoon. Her senses were overloaded.

"Is it any good?" she whispered to Vikki, leaning into the chair with careful movements. The warm island air had brought relief to her stiff joints, and though she felt a lot better and not like a gawky robot on the brink of a fall anymore, she was apprehensive about the session.

"You will love it," Vikki replied, patting her hand.

Sandy willed her muscles to relax. She closed her eyes and hoped for release. The two women masseuses rubbed the spice-infused oils on their flesh with dexterous hands. They used a firmer touch on Vikki, a lighter one on Sandi's sore joints. Tensed fascia slackened and turned to putty as the hour went by. When finished with that, the masseuses had them roll over on their stomachs. They stepped on top of the tables and gripped onto a bar strung from the ceiling and pushed into deep spinal tissue with their soles. The weight of their bodies, controlled by their hold on the bar above, loosened every stubborn, sinewy knot.

A while afterward, they stirred from the massage-induced stupor, wrapped themselves in thick robes and sipped some tea. Sandy stretched luxuriously, feeling renewed, and Vikki sat back with a contented sigh.

Moments later loud voices from the reception area interrupted their conversation. They set their cups on the console and raised their brows at each other in a question mark. It was so unlike the usual calm at the spa that it got their attention. They glanced around wondering what had happened, but the women had left the room. One came in soon after, her expression shaded with fear.

"A body washed in with the tide," she said. She rushed out the room again.

They joined the band of anxious spa employees gathered at the shore for a closer look. The huddled form of a female body topped by a towel lay near a parked police van. Her long hair spilled over on the sands, and an exposed foot had bulbous toes with brightly painted nails. The hollows under the fabric showed the body missed parts. When a breeze lifted the cloth off the dead woman, Vikki gasped with horror. She looked at Sandy who appeared too stricken for words. They had both recognized the whole and intact face. She was the gangling man's companion on Bolim beach.

The cops covered the body. They waved their batons high and herded the onlookers from the scene.

"*Chalo! Chalo!* Move on, everyone, move on!" they said.

"What a horrible end to a life. But not surprising," Sandy said, as they walked away.

"I saw her with another grifter on the beach," Vikki said.

"Drug peddlers," Sandy said.

She pressed her lips tight in a stiff, humorless smile, but her eyes were filled with sympathy for the dead woman.

Chapter 34

Herb glanced back to see how far they had come. Margosa appeared to be a blur from where they stood, he said to Claudia. His comment had her checking the pedometer. They crossed the four-mile mark she said to him with the widest of grins.

"What a difference a year makes," Claudia said to him happily.

"I could walk another ten miles," Herb said to her. He laughed and told her he was ready to continue until they finished.

A year ago, they had signed up for a yoga class to relieve stress and shed a few collective pounds. The sessions were her idea, and Herb had gone along with the plan, but with little zeal. He liked the yoga sessions well enough, he had to admit. They did unwind him after being in a bottleneck for hours on the freeway. And he liked their daily walks which had made both fitter. But their new diet? Not so much.

Claudia assembled a salad for him at lunch. She experimented with plant-based dinners. And though he tried, the meals left him hungry and irritable. Since neither of them cared for strict diets or pills with scary side effects, her sensible plan seemed on track. But Herb was close to breaking.

One afternoon on his way to the mailbox, he bumped into his neighbor, Partho. He mentioned their recent lifestyle shifts and his struggles with the program.

"I have just the cure for you," Partho said. He sifted through his mail and located a brochure with a charming atoll pictured on it. "This is Fins Island. My cousin Selvam manages a spa called Margosa here. Claudia and you go. Relax. Make a vacation out of it."

"Sounds nice and all, but I have operational reports due."

Partho peered at him.

"When did you last travel on break?" he asked.

Herb, looking blank, honestly could not remember.

"About time, then," Partho said, handing him the mailer.

Herb showed Claudia the brochure, and she lit up at the thought of going to the dreamy island. She said a retreat there would be fun, reminding him that they had weeks of unused paid leave. This time around Herb went along with enthusiasm. He was on board with the whole tropical resort getaway thing. What was not to like?

A week into it by now, they reveled in the island's invigorating air, and the expanse of the beach and the sea. The slow pace hinted a day with over twenty-four hours was in front of them. With plenty of chances to do nothing. Though rusty, they switched to vacation mode and put work on the shelf.

Fishermen with wind-worn hands mended their nets by the seashore. They weaved and stitched with a painstaking precision. Children carried sopping buckets of brined shrimp, baby octopi and squid, and hung the slippy creatures on ropes with wood pegs. Whiffs of sea salt and fish guts punctuated the air. The monsoons were nearing, marking the twilight of the trawling season. Fishing boats idled during the rains, and the sundried-to-a-crisp salted tidbits were for those lean times.

As they turned to leave the fishing hamlet, a disheveled man with a bag clutched at his chest ran straight into them. Startled, they jumped apart and let him pass through. Two men followed the runner. The men toyed with him for a bit and pulled at his bag, but he stuck on to it somehow. The three of them scuffled to the ground.

A short distance away were a group of blubs, the professional weepers of the island. The blubs were singing and dancing for their supper at a beach house. A nonagenarian member of the house had died that morning, and the blubs were there to mourn on behalf of the family at the death ceremony. It was considered good luck.

Friends and neighbors who were at the home for the function noticed the scuffle between the three, and they had begun to drift off to watch the fight. The blubs were losing their audience and any tips to be had, and this upset Thesp the lead blub a great deal. He felt slighted, and he flew into a rage.

Thesp rolled up his shirtsleeves and took his wristwatch off and handed it to his assistant. The rest of the blubs followed Thesp. They cracked their knuckles at the brawlers, the usual tactic when they meant business. Thesp ordered them to move on, or the blubs would curse them to eternity with their black tongues.

"We crack you like this! Give you knuckle sandwich," Thesp said, bizarrely twisting his knuckles nearly out of joint.

Right about then the family brought the body out for a viewing. They told the blubs to end their *nautanki*, their silly sideshow, and focus on grieving for the dead. The chastened blubs simmered down. The crowd came back to the home to watch the blubs beat their chests and tear at their hair in faux agony. And the three scuffling men went off to the side and disappeared behind a row of shoreline trees.

Herb held Claudia's elbow in a tight grip. He steered her forward, and away from the drama. They were not sticking around, he told her.

"Not a word. We do not want to mess with them, Dee," he said.

"Maybe we should call the cops," she whispered.

Claudia was sorry for the victim and wanted to help. She punched at the buttons on her cell phone and tried to call the emergency number for police, but the line was busy. Her call did not go through.

At Herb's insistence, they kept moving toward the beach's picnic area ahead and paused there for an interval. When they returned an hour later, the men had gone, and uniformed police officers patrolled the shore. The blubs lounged about under a tree, absorbed with grooming rituals. They were threading the fuzz on their faces with vigor, and real tears streamed down their faces as each hair got yanked from its root.

The balmy evening had drawn people out of their homes and hotel rooms. And the beach looked full of life, different from when they started. Footprints patterned the sands to and from the water where children and adults splashed in the warm surf. Up the waterfront's sandy incline, the restaurants beckoned with neon signs. *"Hot Goyan Pomfret," "Pork Sorpotel," "Mutton Vindaloo"* they announced. Couples enjoying a night out flocked to candlelit tables that were set thick together by a line of popular bars.

Chapter 35

The largest shantytown in Vanati was about five miles south of Bolim, in a dip at the base of the hills. It was an eyesore and a blight on the hilly landscape. This was where most of the thieves, scammers, and those scraping by from day to day on the island lived. Tinnu Chacha owned all of the land and the matchbox sized homes. And when hard up tenants ran out of rent money they paid him with blood, sweat and tears. One way or other they paid.

A nameless alley veered between the lodgings and ended at a corrugated hut. The slanting front door of the hut was barely supported by two of its three hinges. Flat rocks pinioned heavy tarping laid out on the roof. The rocks and tarp were a defense against the monsoon winds and rain that landed with a vengeance every year.

Sec placed his ear at the front door and listened for a minute before knocking on the door. Thak, a Laraban islander with an angular face, held a large backpack and stood next to Sec.

"It's open!" a voice yelled.

Thak prodded Sec through the doorway.

At a table in the one room inside, Tinnu Chacha was busy dismantling his handgun. He flicked a brief glance upwards, and then he paused for a second and aimed the muzzle at them. When he saw their nervous glances, he had a maniacal laughing fit. His upper lip stretched across his metal canines which made him look freakish and unearthly.

Chacha's original name had become lost in time. And since he always referred to himself in the third person, it appeared he had forgotten it too. His first name was a nod to his metal teeth. And the word 'chacha' meaning uncle, was a cutting dig at him by those he had rubbed the wrong way. He acted benign outwardly like your dearest uncle, but it was an act, the opposite of his true self, and part of a clever facade that masked a vicious core. The facade fractured when he was thwarted, and it did today when he saw Thak and Sec.

Chacha never talked of his origins and nobody else dared either. At least not to his face. And people filled the gaping holes in his life story with gruesome anecdotes about him behind his back. Chacha was the deadly uncle you wanted dead, they said of him. If you crossed him he would cut you in pieces, cook your flesh off, and bury the bones in your backyard. Whether he did or not was anybody's guess. He merely jeered at them, used the stories as kindling, and carried on with his trade.

There was one confirmed fact about Chacha. That he had arrived on the island eight years earlier with no cash in hand. And that in a brief period he had established himself as the fattest charas dealer in town.

His turf was limited. He had a ten-mile stretch of territory ranging from Vanati, past Bolim and on toward neighboring Dona Marina. But he had avoided serious trouble by sticking to his area and by dealing in charas alone. It was a drug of slight interest to the big guns like the Russians who had cornered the cocaine market, the Israelis who sold party drugs like ecstasy and ketamine, and the East Europeans who controlled crack. And though certain zip codes on the island were ticking bombs that burst into violence often, the armed dealers sustained an uneasy truce for the most part.

Chacha kept out of it. He was considered small fry anyway and snubbed by the rest. His trade's biggest obstacles were the island cops whom he bought with regularity. The cogs in his operations spun easier because of the bribes he fed the beat cops.

Chacha screwed a bore brush onto a cleaning rod, never taking his eyes off the men.

"Did you find the bastard?" he asked placidly, but with a sneer on his face.

"There were too many people, Chacha. It was not safe," Thak said.

"Chacha is the one in danger! This hero-to-zero Sec cannot manage his woman or his business. Am I safe, asshole?

"We will talk to Fereira."

"Your chacha took care of it, you mouth-breathing snail! He has bribed that dog Fereira to keep this fiasco quiet. Do you know how much?"

He rushed at Sec who stumbled face down. A trickle of blood slid down his mouth where his teeth nicked his tongue. Then Chacha returned to the table and resumed oiling his weapon as if nothing had happened.

"We got Sec's stash. But, like I said, the money's gone," Thak said, his words fading as he spoke.

"Chacha should have killed you at the house. He just might if he does not get his money," Chacha said to the fallen Sec.

Thak held out the backpack as a conciliatory offering, and Chacha snatched it from him and turned the bag upside down.

"What makes you sure this vagrant has our cash?" he said to Thak.

He counted the sealed bags that spilled out the opening.

"He is new in these parts. And Sec caught him dealing on our turf. He may have seen him do away with Sabine, then stole the cash from her," Thak said.

Chacha flung the empty bag at him.

"Tell that dog at Bolim police station Chacha has been robbed. That the woman has gone missing. And blame the asshole who slipped from your hands," he said.

As the men backed off, he reached for an old tire iron at the wall and struck Thak a blow on the anklebone. The Laraban crumpled in agony beside Sec.

"Get out, you filthy swine! Get out!" Chacha screeched.

Sec and Thak clung to each other and limped outside.

Chapter 36

"I am hungry, Herb. Are you?" Claudia said, slipping her arm through his.

"Sure am. For a cheeseburger. And a wedge of lemon meringue," he said.

"We are almost there, Herb," she said cheerfully, surprised by his admission.

"I am doing my best Dee, but it ain't easy," he said, wishing he had her fortitude.

It was not about the food as such. In fact, it was rather good. The resort took great pains to come up with an interesting menu and their creative chefs cooked dishes from scratch daily. It was just that Herb wanted the familiar. He longed for the simple foods he devoured while young. Portions of meat, a helping of starch and a crisp salad. That was all he fancied.

They strolled from the studio to their rooms in silence. Claudia went to freshen up before lunch, and with her out of the room, he turned jumpy. He called to her and said he was off for a walk on the beach while she got ready. She loved soaking in a bath and would barely notice he was gone. It gave him plenty of time, and if everything proceeded according to plan, he would be back by the hour.

At the beach, the aroma of meat on coals and the tang of spices whetted his appetite. He did a slow meander by restaurants with bold names. A promising one named the Sizzle showed a longish non-vegetarian menu. He scanned the day's specials on the chalkboard, and it pleased him to see a Tandoori Tuesday fest happening that day. Tandoor-grilled meats were his favorite Indian food.

The restaurant hopped with customers and every table was taken, but he snagged himself a place at the bar. He waved at a rushing waiter, and he ordered a tray of assorted meat, garlic naan and a chilled brew. When his order arrived, he took a big gulp of the soda.

"That hit the spot," he said to himself, smacking his lips.

He turned at a crashing sound and watched a drunk slide to the floor with his drink in hand. A gasp from the tables, and then all fell to a standstill. The poor bastard, Herb thought, dipping a charred drumstick into the coriander chutney.

Servers crowded about the buckled man. They propped him against a chair and sprinkled icy water on his face to revive him. The Sizzle's owner ran up to the bunch and they helped the man up and dropped him under the shade of a palm tree outside the restaurant.

Herb observed the drunk through the window, ruminating as he ate his meal. He was thinking he might have bumped into him someplace on the island. It came to him then, and he realized where he had seen the guy. The scuffle on the beach the previous afternoon. It was the runner with the bag.

The owner, Al Delgado, approached his table as he was sitting closest to the drunk. He apologized for the commotion, and he offered him another soda for free. Herb had his jaws crammed with garlicky naan and was bursting at the seams already. He waggled his head and declined. Looking at the bones on his plate, he felt content and somewhat guilty. He checked his phone. An hour had gone by since he left on a culinary escapade. He was so full, lunch with Claudia presented a problem.

Meanwhile, Claudia was seated at the table in the dining hall and had started with her cauliflower soup. He bent and kissed her cheek.

"You must be famished, dear," she said to him. "The soup is yummy."

Herb mumbled a suitable response, relieved she suspected nothing, and he rolled up to the buffet. At the serving station, he picked two mango cubes, a slice of melon, and tossed in four grape tomatoes as an afterthought.

"Is that all you are eating, Herb?" she said, glancing at the paltry fare on his dish when he returned.

"I am not too hungry, Dee," he said, avoiding her probing gaze.

He poked at his food and speared a few bites with a fork. Though his hunger had evaporated, he carried on a show of eating anyway. Every morsel he nibbled added to his discomfort until he became sick. He set his fork on the plate and admitted defeat. By evening he came down with a case of severe heartburn. He paced the room and patted his belly for relief which did not help one bit. The front office delivered ginger ale and antacids to the room which did him no good either. When Claudia suggested a wander by the sea in clean air might ease his symptoms, Herb agreed with her.

The Sizzle moved in top gear as they cruised by, and the tables were brimming with tourists. He saw the drunk who collapsed at the restaurant before had not shifted from where servers dumped him. He lolled against the palm, and his head bobbed and jerked like a puppet on a string. Whatever he drank earlier had wiped him out.

Bored urchins pelted the man with sand until a server from the Sizzle had them skedaddle elsewhere. Mica flecks had fused to his grimy skin and sparkled on his hair, and he brushed at his arms and legs in a frenzy to get rid of the sand. He sucked his cheeks and pretended to smoke, holding an imaginary cigarette at his mouth. The passersby hung around and gawked at him, but he seemed not to care.

Herb stopped to watch the man. His behavior reminded him of that one night on the town with friends in his final year. All of them were falling over drunk on the way back. Two of his mates had vomited into the bushes and vowed never to touch a drink again. They whined and groaned, completely out of it. One of his hardier friends had held his liquor admirably well, and he got a bag full of trippy mushrooms out from his jacket pocket.

"I dare you whiners to try some," he taunted, brandishing the baggie at the group.

His roommate was too drunk to know any better. He took up the challenge and scarfed down the entire lot.

The combination of the alcohol and magic fungi was lethal, and it sent him on a dangerous trip. When his girlfriend found him hallucinating in the morning, she rushed him to the hospital. Doctors pumped out his gut, hooked him to an IV, and injected him with an antidote in a final attempt to save his life, but were pessimistic about the outcome.

Lucky for him, he survived the ordeal.

Herb recollected how he had rubbed his limbs that fateful day, much like the drunken man was doing. His actions mirrored the roommate's in such striking ways, he could not tear himself away.

"It could be those spicy beans at dinner, Herb," said Claudia in her thoughtful manner.

She blinked at him. A startled Herb twitched and widened his eyes as if he never saw her before. She wondered if he was doing okay. He acted so strangely of late.

"Have you listened to a word I have said?" she said. And she shook his arm until she had his attention.

Chapter 37

The urchins regrouped and followed Berto. They teased him with insults, speeding as close to him as they dared to see his reaction. When he ignored them, the mob switched to play. He rested and they did too. He walked and the urchins did the same. Berto then gave chase. The yelping imps charged at the ocean to escape, running with the knobby knees and elbows of awkward animals. He yelled, splashed into the surf and pulled faces at them. Soon their attention got diverted by something more amusing than his buffoonery, and they fled and let him be.

He watched them run. Then he waded out and rushed into the cover of the grove. An initial line of trees separated the grove from the rest of the beach and his hideout lay crosswise of that division, within the latter part of the huddle.

The trees grew thick here, and when darkness came the shadows grew thicker than the trees. Wood fires heated pots spotty with meager food and the flames flashed between the branches and washed-up driftwood. People with famished appearances guarded the pots from under torn sheets hung over brush. The cloth shelters were mere coops and functioned as a kitchen and lodging for the night.

As he went along, shiftless drifters and addicts lounged about the thorny scrub. Empty liquor bottles and drug paraphernalia littered the sands. He swerved past them with his head held down, and he kept his distance. A thoughtless word or a look from him could drive the zombies in the crowd into a rage. With deadly consequences for him.

And anyways, his own problems preoccupied him. He had no time to think of other stuff.

The previous tide had flooded the coast with empty crab shells, and Berto ran without a care on the broken bits in his haste to make it to the grove. He sloped as he ran, intent on getting to his buried stuff under the misshapen tree. Once there, he leaned onto the wide trunk and took a break.

An hour later, the sun inched over the sea, dyeing the waters gold-red.

The dusk brought out a mad-eyed crowing woman with dingy hair who fell upon him. She tugged at his shirt and begged him for a smoke. He shoved at her and cursed, and she caught his words and flung them back at him, echoing his curses, mocking him. And then she strayed toward the rickety tents to be with her kind.

The darkness turned deeper once night had fallen. He felt safe in the dark, and he dug under the crooked tree and grabbed the canvas bag out of the earth. The rolls of money yet there in the pockets reassured him. He would leave for Goi and repay his gambling debts, he babbled to himself. And he would return to his usual haunts and watering holes. He wanted his regular brand of feni. His standard plate of No. 24 batter-fried pomfret at the Kingfisher was the best ever. And he dearly missed the place he called home.

He put the bag back into the hole and hid it with dirt. A wave of sleep came over him and feeling lightheaded he settled into the solidness of the broad bole. He tipped his head and closed his eyes. Within seconds of falling asleep, a tightness gripped his chest, and his ribs rattled and cinched in a vice. The air was squeezed from his lungs, and he became unconscious.

Stirring awake in a while, he thought bugs with trembling filaments had crawled over him as he slept. He stood up and brushed them away. Then he stamped into them till they were pulp. He was brushing and stamping at nothing, but he imagined he had conquered his tormentors. There was an immediate rush to his brain as he straightened up, and he felt a victor's euphoria arise in him. He howled at the sky, a beast with his spoils.

At sunrise, he lurched through the open gates of Margosa and went in. The drone of a mower sounded from beyond the lawn. By a row of bushes, the *plink plink* of drops from a leaky hose soaked the ground. He paused at a gap in the undergrowth and scooped up the sludgy mud until he was coated with clay. "Where is it? Where is it?" he said to himself with a ferocious whisper, and that he must retrieve whatever he had lost.

His desperate attempts to find his precious treasure had come to nothing. He told himself it was gone for good. And going far from the noises in the yard, he stumbled into the woods and collapsed on the tangled roots of the trees. The layer of vegetation on the forest floor shifted under his body. He slid around, clutching at a handful of leaves, and he piled them on to keep warm.

His vision was hazy, but he could see his swollen palms. He could see them float away from and to his body. They were stained black and purple like the appendages of a jungle ghoul, and the sight of them sent his heart racing. His ears filled with a deafening roar, and as the end came a light exploded inside him striking him blind. It was over, then.

A coarse dusting of blue salt dropped on him from the treetops. He never heard the rasp of calloused feet slide down a tree trunk. A hand drew his chin upward and exposed the underside of his jaw. Not a single blood drop showed as the dagger's edge swept across his neck and etched a pattern. His heart had stopped dead long before the blade split skin.

Chapter 38

He walked along the shallow brook that ran between the embankments on either side. Tall giants with massive roots rose from the slopes and cast a saturated shade on the forest floor. The dense trees with moss on bark, the curly grass and the tassel ferns reminded Pravesh of his buried past. The land had the same elusive draw.

He had spent years in similar forests in the northeast with a ragtag guerilla group who wanted their own state. The violent separatists had lived by the skin of their teeth. They ambushed travelers, stole any valuables to be had, and escaped into the woods with the pickings. Their separateness, and a gnawing hunger from a constant shortage of supplies, made them malevolent. Carnage in the name of a cause was what they did.

After months on the run, army officers raided rebel hideouts one night and arrested the lot. The state charged him with endangering national security, and he was given the maximum. Fifteen years in the vilest penitentiary in the country for his crimes.

He paused for a minute to clear his head, and he continued on to his choice spot. It was a haven he had found earlier, a thinking spot on a mound of tufted grass. When he got there he came across Sandy with her camera aimed at the treetops, and he waved at her to be friendly, but she did not see him. A little vexed by her being there, he climbed the embankment toward higher ground in search of solitude.

Sandy scrolled the images on the screen. She was taken by how the lush jungles exploded with birds of every color. Her camera and a bird anthology came with her on these daily jaunts, and she took pictures every chance she had.

An oriole, near but invisible, sang again. A gold and black spark from inside a jamun tree and off he flew, his song as lucid as pattering rain. Steps further, she saw a pied bunting. A flycatcher. And then a nest of newborn spotted owls that had her smiling for joy.

Out of the corner of her eye, she noticed a fluttering above a bush. A flicker of a shadow, and then a bird's tail plumes fanned out over the top of the scrub against the light. Rays flowed through the strands setting alight the orbs at their tips. She drew in her breath, not believing her eyes. Was that an Orbed Salten she was seeing? She went through the book, rustling the pages until she came to the shape shifting birds of paradise. This was the bird in the bush. The Orbed Salten, a bird that was extinct for more than a century. Last viewed on Fins Island in 1901, the description said. How could that be?

She adjusted her lens and zoomed in, but she had missed her chance. Her wide-eyed stare jumped from the empty space above the scrub and back to the image on the page. The bird was gone. Disappointed with herself, she packed her gear and headed out to the trail. She wished she had been quicker with her camera.

A mile away, up on the embankment, Pravesh rested in a grove of neem trees. The world receded from him, became inconsequential. He lost all sense of time. Then a hard sound split the quiet and rang for a second, breaking the spell. He heard a stealthy crepitation at the base of the trees. The foreign noise was uncommon in the woods, and it bothered him enough that he tiptoed his way to the embankment's edge for a look.

Below him, a stick-like figure scratched at the roots with dirt-encrusted hands. Rain clouds rolling by the forest revolved overhead, and an unexpected clap of thunder disturbed the man. He stared at the trees and turned his head around in degrees, as if watching for something. During a lull in the skies he limped forward and resumed scraping at the damp rot that covered the woodland floor. Pravesh inched backwards from the edge and left before the man discovered his presence.

Chapter 39

G *oi* The posh enclave of brick and glass buildings had no number plates or names. Bulldog law firms with a long list of celebrity clients spanned entire blocks at the gated reserve, and the more influential the firm the greater was its mass.

A maze of hallways and rows of unmarked doors were disorienting, and newcomers were often lost until a phone call brought staff to their rescue. Souza was there for a meeting with his lawyer whose office lay somewhere in that labyrinth. But he knew his way around by now.

He had a fair idea of the worth of his discovery. The floor plans in the family library showed a belowground vault system built on what was now Souza land. It had sprung from a vision of Souza's ancestor Mohun Garé, the Samudri king's vizier and right-hand man.

The city was constructed to hold and protect the kingdom's colossal wealth.

Granite vault doors were submerged in a passageway of water tunnels that ran all the way to the sea. Brakar sharks, a sightless species of shark, lived in the waterways and fed on the bait sentries threw in the dark waters. The only safe access to be had on dry land was through a trapdoor in the king's palace that led to a hatch inside the vaults. Opening the sealed stone doors in the tunnels would be deadly, to say the least. It had to give looters pause for thought.

In the vaults, the record said, were the riches of the famously rich king and his heirs. Chests of gold and silver coinage minted by the royal treasury for his many pitiless wars. And the precious loot and plunder from the kingdoms he had won and annexed. Then there were a ton of donations of gems and lavish jewelry given to the vanquisher king by his new subjects as proof of allegiance to him.

Not to mention the artifacts and heirlooms passed on by Souza's family that were stored in the vaults for safekeeping.

Souza believed the records were true. He had heard comparable stories as a child, and he yet remembered them. His brother shared those memories too, and this had become his biggest concern. But he thought the law had an answer to his problem.

The answer was in Berto's history, which Souza knew like the back of his hand.

Berto's first foray into crime began on the night of his eighteenth birthday. He broke into a relative's empty house on that night and stole some cash and valuables from a safe. Months afterward, the swiped relics had turned up in the underground markets of Panji.

The family he stole from never reported the crime out of concern for them but cut off all social contact. It had come as a terrible shock to their parents, and their poor mother had wept for days after the incident became known.

Berto was still the cut and run artist. And Souza had always been the one to pick up the pieces and put him together. His most recent disappearing act gave Souza cause to move the law in his favor now. A case of legal incompetency filed against Berto in the state's bureaucratic courts would buy him time. While the lawyer fought on his behalf, his work with Lala could begin, and by then Berto would be out of the picture.

"We made a startling find this past week, Batti," he began as soon as he entered the room. "You may recall the Samudri king's vault city an earthquake buried centuries ago?"

"Certainly. It was an underground city. If memory serves me right."

"It was. Well, the recent quake has unburied it. A reverse fault generated an upthrust. They could not have known at the time, but it was built on a fault. The Forge Fault. Which runs through my land, of course."

He strummed his fingers on the desk and watched for the lawyer's response. Batti was equable, but a nerve jigged at his earlobe.

"Have you told Berto?" he asked Souza.

"He is nowhere to be found! May be dead for all I know.

"It is on jointly held land."

"Who gives a damn?"

"This is exciting news," a straight-faced Batti said. "Of great historical value to Goi. And I daresay the country. We can issue a public statement if you wish."

"Hold off for the present."

"Certainly."

"I want Berto declared legally incompetent first before we go public."

The canny lawyer peered over his readers at Souza.

"If you so prefer," he murmured.

"He is a distraction I can do without."

"Understandable."

"Aside from that, I am most keen on starting excavation."

The lawyer steepled his fingers, looking contemplative.

"Did you know under the Treasures Act of 1797 –"

"What about it?"

"Ancient artifacts unearthed on private land belong to the state. Section 204, para vii," Batti said.

Souza stood up, his manner flinty.

"What does that outdated law have to do with Berto?" he said.

"Oh, nothing."

"The law is worthy of the dung heap."

"An inconvenient law in your case," Batti said with a laugh.

"Stick to what you know. File the declaration of incompetency," Souza snapped. "It must be on my desk for review tomorrow morning.

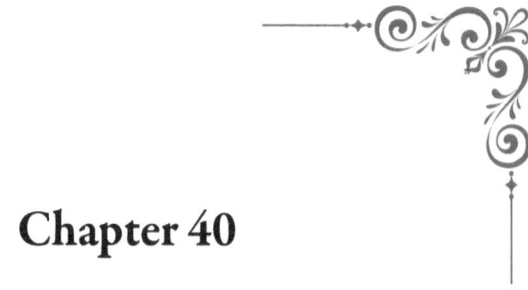

Chapter 40

ins Island

F Naini's heart skipped a beat in anticipation when she turned the corner, but the verandah was empty. She paused at a bench by the pathway, and she removed a fresh betel leaf from the metal box in her bag. Then she dug out a bit of slaked lime and smeared it at the leaf's side. She dropped pieces of areca nuts in the center, folded it into a neat parcel, and placed the tiny envelope on her tongue. The spicy concoction stung the roof of her mouth in a tingling rush. She chewed slowly for a while.

She put her things away, and stepping off the path, she went into the cover of the forest to relieve herself. At the embankment below, she stopped and squatted behind a tree. When she stood once more a monstrous fly landed on her arm and she swatted at it hard. The peeved fly buzzed and flew in circles before it rested on a fur scrap lying on top of a leaf pile.

Curious, she picked up a fallen branch and brushed aside the hairy debris from the pile. What she discovered underneath revolted her and made her ill to her stomach. Overcome by what she was seeing, she sank into the mud. She pressed her fists against her teeth to suppress a scream. Berto Souza lay unmoving under the decayed vegetation. Moldering rot shrouded his eyes, his open jaws. The other corpse flies hidden inside his decomposed flesh became cross at her poking around and they swarmed over the remains in a whirl. That he would never bother her again overwhelmed her until she shook. Naini clambered up the slippery embankment, and she emerged out of the woods and hurried toward Margosa.

The evening had faded, spent its color, but a warm glow from the dining hall windows was now coming through. Snippets of conversation mixed with the unhurried clinks of cutlery on plates meant dinner service had begun.

She pulled spiky burrs off her clothing and waited for everything to wind down for the night.

Chapter 41

Bolim was the final destination for public buses from Goi to the island, and Kelkar decided to start at the local police station there. The town's habitual criminals sat outside on a bench waiting to be booked and he moved past them and went inside. Officer Savio Fereira was the person in charge at the station. Of middling height, puffy featured, he did not conceal his animus when he saw him.

"You want access to our police logs," Fereira said thinly, reaching for a toothpick from a tray. He slid it between his teeth, looking busy and indifferent at the same time.

His disdain, glazed with a brittle veneer of hostility, did not surprise Kelkar. He had encountered that attitude in his previous interactions with island cops: he sort of expected it.

"Any pertinent information is helpful," Kelkar said.

"Not much happens out here in Bolim. Maybe a handful of petty larceny during the year. And then we have the usual domestic disputes," Fereira said, after a tedious delay.

"Not from what I hear. You have the mundane problems we do in Goi. Illegal drugs and corrupt cops," he retorted.

"One cannot escape being human. If you understand what I am saying," Fereira said with a crafty wink at him.

"Shall we get on with it?" he said stonily.

Fereira grated on him. He smelled like a rotten cop.

"Of course, of course," Fereira said, leading him to the documents section. "We will do our best to help in this matter. But I must warn you, nothing much has happened these last few weeks. It is one boring day after another."

"We can pass on a few cases. Make it exciting for you."

"You can sh—-," Fereira began to say.

Fereira sorely lacked humor, and he felt sorry for the deputies at the station.

Cabinets lined the records room on all four sides, with rows of tables and chairs in the center. He signed on to the department computer at a corner table and began with the daily police logs.

If an officer responded to a disturbance and arrested a suspect, he filed an arrest report. If no arrest occurred, the officer classified it as an incident report. They saved both types on a computer with a paper copy filed in the cabinets.

He opened with the days prior to when Berto might have landed on the island.

The lists had disturbances common to most towns. First, a store robbery. Then two wacky neighbors up in arms over their pets. The same day, an accidental drowning of a British tourist. Then a threatening ex of an ex. Some sporadic animal abuse. He reread an incident report about a fracas involving three men on Bolim beach. Police responded an hour after the phone call. When they arrived, the men had gone.

He printed the single sheet of paper and stepped out the room to show it to Fereira.

"Did you ever follow up on this?" he asked.

Fereira's face split in an unctuous smile. He pulled the toothpick out of his teeth with a gargling sound and ran his eyes over the report.

"Look here, Kelkar," he said, pushing the sheet away. "People travel to India on student visas, get to these parts and sell drugs. Bolim has too many incidents like these. We cannot patrol every beach. It is impossible. The person beaten up did not contact police, so we let it pass. This drug dealing riffraff can kill each other for all I care."

"Were they local or from elsewhere on the island?" Kelkar pressed him.

An annoyed Fereira flung his arms up in the air.

"People arrive and go as they please," he said. "Look here, Kelkar, I have work to do. And I suggest you let me do my job."

"Thought you said nothing much happens here."

"Things crop up, even here in Bolim."

"By the way, you were about fifteen minutes from the scene. Your guys showed an hour after. Do you know why?"

"Traffic is bad some days."

"Did the witness describe the individuals?"

"It is all in the report. The caller witnessed two men thrashing another person. He provided no specifics."

"Thanks. Till we meet again."

Fereira popped his paunch out over his belt.

"Good luck with the case," he said. "And try our jackfruit feni before you return. It is far superior to Goyan cashew feni."

"I don't drink. Will take your word for it, though," Kelkar replied.

He walked out, and two men passed him and went into the station. One of them, an angular-faced Laraban, had a loose bandage wrapped round his ankle. The other was an emaciated man with a mass of sandy hair under a hat. A stripe of dried blood scuffed his chin. He shuffled sideways with a crooked gait, smacking into his companion as he climbed the stairway. Both appeared to have been in a bruising fight.

He waited in a cafe across the street for them to finish their business. When his phone beeped with an incoming text, he snatched a quick glance at the screen.

"Did you read the news today?" text from Rego read.

About fifteen minutes later the two came out of the station and he followed behind. Fereira knew more about the squabble in the report than he admitted. His hunch had steered him right. He sensed it in his bones.

Chapter 42

Staff heard the cries halfway through their monthly meeting. The sounds sprung them from their seats and straight to the door. Tara thought it might be connected to the earlier break-in at the conservatory, and she exchanged a worried glance with Selvam as she hurried after the rest.

They ran around the building to see a distraught Sandy on the pathway. Vikki, who was with her, was trying to calm her down.

"She says she saw a dead man there," Vikki said to them, pointing to the woods.

She now saw the scene with Sandy's eyes. Dangers lurked close, and she wondered how safe they were.

"Call Bolim police," Ronnie Barbosa said to Jha, pulling him aside.

Fereira arrived at the site, and he waved the loitering workers away. Soon after his coming, the lead investigator and photographer drove up in a staff van. The two geared up, progressing in a slow arc towards the scene and searching for clues on the soggy ground.

A thick layer of humus cloaked a corpse lying on a bed of leaves. The investigator brushed the debris off the surface and removed a wet leaf from an eye socket with his gloved finger. Fereira walked back with a gagging heave.

"Berto Souza," the investigator said to him.

"Are you sure?" Fereira said, stepping forward to check.

He gawped with his palm cupped over his nose.

"Sure as can be. Wasn't he missing?"

"A detective from Goi is looking for him."

"No ID on the body. But I am certain it is the guy."

Dr. Deb Sahu, the island's medical examiner, came by and waited for them to wrap up. Fereira traded snarky glances with the team and made a motion behind the doctor's back.

"He's started early today," Fereira said with a low snicker. They laughed discreetly between them.

When the photographer got done, the doctor stepped up to the body. The remains had softened, grown lax, with flabby green skin bubbling in blisters under torn clothing. Blood had pooled in purplish blotches under the extremities. A quick look told him the death occurred less than forty-eight hours ago. He examined the feet and hands. Then he sketched rough images of the victim in his journal. He wrote and drew for the next hour. Once he completed his examination, lab technicians, the drudge personnel from his office, trudged in. They would wind up with fingerprints and any trace evidence before they compiled team reports.

The doctor scrubbed off with disinfectant at the van's station.

"Find any dead animals near the body?" he asked the investigator.

"None within a hundred-foot radius," the investigator replied.

"Widen the search. If you discover any, send those to me. They are important."

"How do you think he died?" Fereira asked the doctor with a tacky familiarity.

"You will know after I complete the autopsy," the doctor said, leveling a withering stare at him.

It had been four hours since the death scene investigation began. The clouds above the treetops were leaden. Heavy raindrops fell like buckshot, gathered speed, and crashed into the trees in staccato bursts. The overflow spattered the earth, and in minutes rivulets swept down the embankments and joined the rollicking stream.

"Come on everyone! Bag that body before the skies open up!" the investigator yelled out to lab technicians.

The doctor moved with exaggerated care past the anxious employees waiting for news. Fereira kept his gaze on him. Then he reached for his phone to make a call.

Chapter 43

The two men tramped toward an upturned fishing coracle on the sands. There they sat at the boat's shaded side with heads down and their backs to Kelkar. He went past them and to the restaurant ahead to ask around.

"What about those two?" he asked the owner who came up to his table. He gestured at the men.

"Allow me to guess. Goi police?" Al Delgado said with an easy sureness.

Kelkar smiled at his prescience. He introduced himself.

"You own this place?" he asked him.

"For almost ten years and counting. Managed it well, too. But the island has become as bad as Goi - no offense to you."

"You stayed, though."

"We do all right."

"What about them?"

"The thin crook with the crazy hair is Sec, a drug peddler from Spoker. Works this entire stretch from Vanati to Dona Marina. He sells his poison to people on the waterfront but keeps away from businesses here. A common thug, he can be dangerous."

He dropped his voice.

"A woman who followed Sec everywhere like a lost dog washed up dead last week. I still feel the chills when I relive that day. See?" he said, pointing at goose bumps on his arms. "One morning we thought a dolphin had beached on the shore. I sent a waiter to check things out before we phoned the authorities. He ran to look and fainted on his way here. It was Sec's girlfriend. Bloated with water. Half of her flesh eaten by what sea creatures, God only knows. She arrived from across the oceans and died by misfortune here on Bolim beach. That is fate, eh?"

Delgado went on.

"Very suspicious. The woman is with him for months, then they discover her dead. Anyway, the bloke disappeared for a period. And now he is back to peddling on the beach with the Laraban there. He goes by the name of Thak and is in the same racket as Mr. Bag of Bones."

"This person ever come here?" Kelkar asked.

He laid out Berto Souza's photographs.

"Mm-hmm, he has been here," Delgado said. "He rejected the jackfruit feni we had on the menu and wanted Goyan cashew feni instead. We do not sell your feni on the island."

"And we do not sell yours. Against the law in both places."

"You know that, and I know that. When I explained the reason to him politely, he had a fit. This guy was a nuisance, let me tell you. He drank so much beer the other afternoon he fell off his chair. I threw him out so he could get decent."

"I want a word with your staff."

"By all means. I have five full-time attendants here. The only troublemaker among them named Sal has not shown up for days - the scoundrel. But you can talk to the rest."

The staff recognized Berto, but neither they nor Delgado recalled seeing him with the two dealers.

When he asked Delgado who served Berto that day, he returned with his logbook. He searched the pages until he located a date. The good-natured owner, his brow knitted in a furrow, wore an uncustomary scowl.

"Sal Bilbao last waited on him," he said. "I remember because he left that evening. The rascal fled on our busiest night. We were a man short, and I called up my cousin for help. This happened previous Tuesday. I have not seen the missing guy or Sal since."

Chapter 44

" They found a body. Better get here quick," Fereira said to Kelkar over the phone.

The crime lab van parked ahead had its engine idling. Across from it, yellow barricade tape tied around trees marked the space. A body rested on a stretcher next to the van in a mortuary bag, and the impatient attendants stood ready to seal the top and stop for the day. They had held off until he came and identified the body.

When Kelkar arrived, the men lifted the sheeting higher, and he bent low under the plastic and inspected the remains. Disappointment pricked him when he saw a lifeless Berto Souza in the sack. This ending had come sooner than he expected.

He made the final identification and signed off on the forms.

As workers tweaked at the zipper it jammed partway, and the head rolled up before the attachments sealed at the end. He made them stop. There was an inscription, a scar of some type, under Berto's jaw. About four inches long, it resembled a curving vine on both ends and looked rather like an etched design on the skin. He clicked a picture and moved out of their way.

"Does this mean you are finished?" Fereira said.

"Quite the contrary. I start now," he said, taking a certain relish when he detected his annoyance.

"But why?" Fereira spluttered.

Kelkar did not report to anyone on the island. Fereira would get zilch from him.

"Who does the autopsies here?" Kelkar asked, ignoring the question.

"Dr. Deb Sahu. An exceptional forensic pathologist with a drinking problem," he replied. "He chews on cloves to hide the fact. But everybody in the force knows he is an alcoholic."

"When was he appointed?"

"About ten years ago. The Finsian governor handpicked him to lead the crime lab. People say he became a different man after the 2004 tsunami killed his whole family. His father, mother, and a brother were all washed away while they vacationed in Sri Lanka. He has not been the same."

Fereira got into the squad car.

"Need a ride?" he asked.

"You move on. I have to catch up with calls," he said.

He waited until he drove off before calling Souza's office.

"I have bad news," he began.

"What is it?" Souza said.

"They found Berto dead."

There was silence at the other side, and then an exasperated expletive that sounded close to relief.

"How did he die?"

"We cannot be sure until the ME's report is out."

"Not much you can do now."

"I am waiting on the report."

"Let the island authorities figure it out. The last thing I want is the blasted Finsian governor whining about us being pushy. Touchy people, those islanders. Good work but get back soon."

"Will get going then," Kelkar said.

He retraced his steps through marshy mud and toward the death scene. Rain pooled in a depression where the body had lain. A gauzy cloudburst misted and blurred the setting.

He paused on the embankment and glanced at the brook below him. It was now a large rushing stream. The downpours had swelled its volumes, and the swift currents dragged the forest's waste along.

As he stood there lost in thought, the earth under him loosened and dissolved in a wash of silt. He reached for a branch and that's when he saw the lone feather at the end. The downy underside ruffled, and for a moment he felt the wind might knock the feather off its perch. He slid it off the bough. The fronds caught the light and fanned out, and tiny orbs at their points sparked like shimmers on seawater. He gazed up, and he envisioned a resplendent bird that wore these gliding high above the seas. One that soared, wheeled, and never touched terra firma.

He hurried through the torrent of rain to the lodge where he rented a suite. Before he rode the elevator to his rooms on the third floor, he picked a copy of the Times from the rack at the front desk. In his room he leveled out the folds truncating the headline and he scanned the full header.

"Diem supporters attacked at rally," the block of text stated.

A loud group started a stampede at the rally and the crush of crowds had sent a dozen of Diem's people to the hospital, the report said. Ludi Rodrigues and Tips Sattu were identified as the miscreants who instigated the melee. Though they argued that Diem factions incited them, their version rang false to his ears.

He read the article in its entirety and called Rego.

"Those are Lala's men. What were they doing at the rally?" Kelkar said.

"Seems fishy to me, too," Rego agreed. "I tracked Lala. My contact said the guy is flush with money."

"From where?"

"A shady source."

"How did you figure that?"

"He bought an entire jewelry store one day crazy as that sounds. In cash. And he snapped up vast tracts of vacant land on the outskirts of the capital. Again, in cash. Word on the street is he plans to build a syndicate of casinos out in the countryside."

"The area is not zoned for casinos."

"Shall I drive out there and check?"

"No, not yet."

"I hear Berto Souza is dead, sir."

"That is right."

"What comes next?"

"Head out here. We have leads."

The room was musty but cozy and dry. He removed his damp clothes and put on something warm. A sudden hankering for masala chai swept over him. Chai prepared in the manner Rayna did on the days he felt a cold coming. Hot tea with black pepper, ginger, and a touch of honey.

Turns of thunder rolled through the sky, announcing the coming of bad weather. The lightning flashed on the ceiling like a match being struck and extinguished in darkness. He closed the shuddering windows and latched them before an inevitable rain fell. Then he plugged in the kettle. He dropped a spiced tea bag into the mug, and he watched the water bubble to a boil.

Chapter 45

The ravens were a cloud of indignation in the clear sky, rallying the flock with their shrieking cries. Their frenzied behavior puzzled Bir, but he understood why once he spotted the lifeless raven on the walkway. The stiffened bird had innards exposed and was lying in a circle of feathers. Their shouts were a dirge for the dead.

As he hurried past the remains the ravens above turned bolder. They swooped down and pecked him on his head as though he was responsible for the bird's death. He shielded his face with his arms and ran until he reached the studio's safety.

The agitated birds flew overhead for a few minutes and then they were gone.

He picked up a CineFolly magazine from the table. The cover featured a popular movie star draped in a sheer sarong, and with a gummy smile he found appealing. He had a good hour to while away till lunch, and he flipped the lustrous pages, dense with pictures of stars with pomaded hair and chiseled jawlines. His boredom transformed into a breathless expectation as the images blurred into one. He began to see Paroma transposed on every female figure in the magazine.

Later he did his usual detour by the front office, and as he went closer sounds of bantering laughter coasted his way. He thought he heard his name mentioned, and the gossipy remarks distracted him. He lost his balance, slipped on a gory mess on the ground and landed on his back. Bir scrambled to right himself and soon realized he had stepped on the liquefied carcass of a cat.

THE UPTURNING

The animal lay slit open from stomach to jaw like the raven he discovered earlier. He had witnessed two slaughtered animals with similar wounds in a single day, and it would strike anyone as odd under the circumstances. But to Bir it was not odd at all. He was someone who ignored life's coincidences, passing them without a care or thought in the world. The irregularity of the deaths made no impression on him, and he had already forgotten what he had seen by the time he showered and changed.

Chapter 46

Before the incident happened they had usually chatted and exchanged notes at mealtime. The evening after Sandy found the body, things were different as they sat at the table. There was a morose silence in the dining hall at Margosa and not much talk. The familiar bunch of servers in the hall seemed listless too. They were less solicitous of the guests and stood at the buffet loafing around and looking lost. The steam pans meant to hold food stood half-filled or almost empty.

Nobody was watching the local news and the show trundled on the television in the hall with its volume on low. The satellite maps on screen showed the island receding under a whorl of whipped clouds, and a chyron below the picture displayed news of a rare summer hurricane in the coming days. A grave meteorologist on the newscast had a windbreaker on even though he was in the studio.

"Residents must remain indoors and shelter at home," he warned, jabbing at the screen with rattled eyes.

The live coverage cut to a program break, and old video footage of surf rushing up and flooding the span played over and over as if in actual time. Images of abandoned beaches, boarded restaurants and shut-in tourists staring out of black windows haunted the viewer. A vibrant island had assumed the drab look of a ghost town overnight.

The bridge was now under water, and since it was the only land route out stranded travelers had no passage by road anymore. Seas roiled rough, making it impossible to take a boat out either. A wall of waves prevented commercial ferry services to and from the mainland.

The hurricane was hours away and muscling into shore, and the islanders were going nowhere for a while.

The director stepped through the doors of the hall to address the group.

"The unfortunate events at Margosa are troubling," Rish began. "But let me assure you, all safety precautions are in place. Police are on routine patrol outside the gates, and we have our own security guards on constant watch inside the resort. Please enjoy the rest of your visit without worry."

Guests and employees rushed at the director after the briefing. They peppered him with questions but returned to their seats disappointed when he provided no answers. Police had yet to give him a full account on the incident, he told them, and he promised more details as matters developed. He knew as much as they did.

"We should pack up and take off once the hurricane blows over, Herb," Claudia said unhappily. She pushed her dish aside.

"Now, now, no need to get too carried away," Herb said.

He wrapped his arm around her and gave her a squeeze.

"Can one be safe anywhere?" Vikki said. "One day I got on public transport to meet a client in the city. A few seats from me on the metro was a demented guy. Next thing I know, he had stabbed the person beside him. I read they were complete strangers to each other."

"Yeah, but we can leave," Claudia pointed out.

"I admit it freaked me out when I first heard, but I am staying. This is good. Like Rish said, there are security personnel everywhere. And I figure we will be fine. Maybe it was an accident. We do not have the facts," she said. She glanced out the window. "And that, is life. Stuff happens."

The news channel now had clips of immense waves crashing the bridge with those of trees falling on houses. It rolled on the screen in an uninterrupted loop. The same waves crashed, and the same trees fell. Over and over and over again.

Chapter 47

"Look here, Kelkar," he said. "It is best you leave the questioning to us island cops. We have this."

He bristled, resisting an impulse to end the call. Fereira wanted him out before he even started.

"Good morning to you, too," he said.

"We agree you are leaving for Goi, then?"

"Let's wait for the autopsy report before we jump the gun."

"I see what you mean. We do not know how he died."

"Correct."

It rained without reprieve in the following days. Traffic snarls and downed structures were everywhere. Water-logged tree branches snapped, and destroyed cars lined at street curbs. Some ancient trees lost the fight entirely and crashed on rooftops. Emergency calls from citizens who demanded the town remove blockages swamped Fereira and his crew and kept him out of his hair.

Later in the day when he arrived at the resort, Tara described how staff ran outside when they heard shouts. Their public affairs manager had Jha inform police at once, she said. Kelkar wrote himself a mental note to contact the manager Ronnie Barbosa later.

"The weight loss clinic has eight full-time clients enrolled as of now. However, they are sick people. And they stay mostly in bed because of a rigorous fasting schedule. Other than that, we have six visitors at a month-long yoga retreat," she explained.

"Give me the names of the six guests," Kelkar said to her.

She gave him a site map and the list of names.

"Could this be the same person who broke in?" she asked.

"Maybe," he said.

She made a call, and her staff came into the office. He held up Berto's picture for them.

"Seen this guy?" he inquired.

They shook their heads.

"Do any of you know Naini?"

"I hired a janitor by that name," Tara said in a rush.

"Where is she?"

Naini was missing from the group.

"We suspended ground activities because of the weather. I assume she is at the work shed or with Jass, the gardener. Staff can check for you."

"Don't bother. I can find my way there."

The work shed's door stood ajar. He went inside and swept his eyes across the spare interior. The shelves and racks were heaped with crates and cans. Garden tools hung from the hooks on the wall. There was a glass of wilted calendulas in water on the windowsill, and the fragrance of the fading flowers lingered in the dim room. A thick sleeping bag under the window had crinkled snapshots of movie stars and music lyric booklets hidden below the fabric.

He bolted the door and returned to the front office.

Chapter 48

A caption below the vintage photographs read, *"Kori tribals, circa 1875."* The subjects in the pictures stared with an acute suspicion at the camera, as if it might suck out their souls with every smoking flash.

In one of the pictures, a clique of male tribals sat close together while a solitary man sat at a distance from them. The solo tribal held himself very tall. Fine gold chains circled his neck, with jeweled hoops attached to pierced ears. His large, feathered war mask appeared more opulent than what the others had on.

Kelkar picked up a travel book from the wall shelf and started to read about them.

It said the Kori lived on the island in the tenth century, much before the Portuguese settlers arrived east. Kori kept to Fins Island. And an order of fearsome curers, healers with secret knowledge of plants and herbs, ruled the tribe. One of their elixirs had in fact made it to the outside in the seventies, if only briefly.

The island's unspoiled waters were little known to the modern world before that. When word spread about the peak conditions there, mostly from online postings, divers came. And with the divers came more sharks. As the attacks on humans increased, fear kept divers away for a long time.

Then a rumor began on chats of a repellant, some sort of salve Kori used. And it reignited interest in the island. Rumor was sharks never attacked Kori pearl fishers because of it.

But was it true? A visiting diver decided to find out.

After some wheeling and dealing through intermediaries, he persuaded their leader to hand him a sample. He tried the repellant on a few dives and was convinced it worked. But when he asked the secretive Kori what was in there, they refused to say.

That was one of many stories about the Kori.

"Yes, what is it I can be doing for you?" Jha asked walking into the front office.

"We have not met," Kelkar said, introducing himself.

The manager tapped at his chest.

"And myself, I am P. Jha, the all-purpose office manager," he said.

"Cent per cent true stories in book," Jha said when he saw the travel book.

"Is there a tea vending machine here?" Kelkar asked him, putting the book back on the shelf.

"No tea appliance is there. Only homemade tea is present in office. Is tip top."

"Sounds good to me."

"I can utilize a teacup also same time. Bad, this whole dead body business. The Governor's brother, I hear," he tut-tutted. He reached for a thermos on his desk.

Jha handed him a mug of tea.

"Photographs have caught your attendance, I am noticing. Beautiful history of the island in pictures. Guests are liking it too much," he said.

"Odd seating that," he remarked, pointing to the lone tribal figure in the picture.

He took a sip of the milky tea and wished at once for a stronger brew.

"He is medicine man. The tribe call him curer. Powerful, but has tearful story also."

"Why is he not with the rest?"

"No, no, that is dangerous. He can kill with smallest touching as he is eating on special poison from when he is an infant. So his skin and all over is too deadly. He must live alone, elsewhere from bunches of village peoples."

"I have heard ancient myths about women who poisoned with a touch," Kelkar mused.

"These things were only happening over hundred years ago," Jha said. "This poison thing is not chancing anytime now. Outlawed in 1900. But guests are all interested in this picture very much. Why that man is sitting by himself, they ask to me. I have another jokey story for you."

Kelkar smiled.

"I like jokey stories," he said.

"The Governor of Goi was living on Fins Island when he was young. Now his brother is dead on island. Like a completing circle, no?"

"You could say that," he said, surprised by the reveal. He knew sketchy details of Souza's life as a youth. It never came up when they met.

"Yes, yes, it is all-knowing news on the island. Watch out," Jha went on. He drew his attention to a photograph in color of tropical-suited smiling men. "That man with the fulsome beard is Peter Souza before he is becoming big honcho guy. Here he is being youthful and learned man, living with tribals to write thesis. Now you are also learning little bit Goi-Fins connection."

He snorted out a laugh. The phone at his desk rang, and he excused himself.

Kelkar was lost in reverie when he felt a tap on his shoulder.

"Did you talk to her?" a worried Tara asked him.

"She is not at the work shed," he said.

"The gardener Jass has some interesting news," Tara said.

Chapter 49

Selvam moved his box of saplings to the shade and came forward. Kelkar read the names of herbs as they walked the lined beds.

"I can tell this stuff fascinates you," Kelkar said.

"Each tells me a story," Selvam said.

He pinched a verbena leaf and handed it to him.

"Has a medicinal odor," Kelkar said.

"It is medicine. The plants are lifesavers for the sick."

Kelkar smiled.

"All I know about herbs is that mint tastes great in tea," he said.

He brushed past a peppermint bush. The fragrant oils dispersed and sparked a memory, fresh despite the passage of years. A memory of him sipping peppermint tea on a sunny afternoon as rain poured from one darkened end of the sky.

They went on indoors. Selvam described how Naini raced toward the spa after she reported on a stranger. It appeared as if she was running for her life, he said.

"How many employees do you have here?"

"Two chefs who work kitchens, four full-time masseuses, and a receptionist. And then there is the herbalist and me. A head gardener, his assistants, and a janitor, maintain the grounds."

Selvam called the indoor staff in, but none of them knew anything.

He angled the window blinds and rolled up the shade. A noisy troupe of yard workers filed through a gap in the hedge.

"The garden staff are outdoors at all times. You might gather a lot more information from them," he said, looking out the window and waving at them.

Kelkar strolled over to the yard and interrupted their lunch.

"Know where Naini is?" he asked the staff.

They shook their heads.

"Who is the head gardener?"

A rangy man stood up, and Kelkar drew him aside. They headed to where Naini ran into the intruder.

"Here. This is where I cleared empty beer cans and charas packets," Jass said, stopping at a certain point in the dense undergrowth.

"What did you do with the charas?"

Jass was sheepish.

"I will not lie to you. We...,"

"You mean you and your team in the garden?"

"Yes, them. We smoked it."

"I heard you kept an eye on Naini."

"Tara Shaw ordered me to."

"Did you notice she has disappeared?"

Jass clapped a hand to his forehead.

"It has been all topsy-turvy after they recovered the body. I have not seen her since," he said.

Jass inclined his head toward him.

"In fact," Jass continued, glancing about him as if about to reveal a secret. "Naini and Rish Tilak were...."

Kelkar waited.

"Every day, they lay together. I told Tara Shaw everything," Jass said.

"You can go finish your lunch. Go on," he said to him.

In the clearing where Jass had noticed the garbage, a piece of plastic extended out of the earth. Kelkar tugged at it until it broke loose. A square parcel entwined with stretchy bands was buried in the shallow hole. He removed the parcel, slid the bands off the plastic cover and undid the package. Inside, he found a thick bundle of dollar bills; the notes crumpled but crisp.

Chapter 50

The hurricane hit the Crossing the hardest and had cracked the concrete buttresses that supported the deck. City officials inspected the damage and closed the span until it was fixed and safe to travel. On the plus side, the sea had calmed. Ferry services restarted, and crammed boats with people hanging out the open sides dashed in fits from the harbor and to the mainland. The following days on land dawned glorious and sunny and with no winds. Area schools reopened, customers swarmed stores to replenish supplies, and life awakened to more or less normal.

Kelkar got ahead of traffic. He arrived at Margosa early, and while he waited for staff to unlock the rear gates, Fereira drove up in his squad car. He parked, then came around to his passenger side and tossed an envelope through the window. In no hurry, he leaned into the window and picked at his cuticles.

"The autopsy report," he said.

"Okay. Will do," Kelkar said.

"What a hectic week," Fereira declared. "The weather clears, and what do I see?"

"I have the report, Fereira."

"Lowlife criminals crawling out from sewers," Fereira prattled on.

"Bye, now," Kelkar said.

"They do not pay me enough to do this. Give me hell any day," he said, lurking by the car.

He grated, as usual. Kelkar started to roll up his windows and Fereira jerked his arms back before the glass hit.

"You will be gone once you read the report," he yelled as he sped off.

As soon as he tore the package top, his phone rang.

"Well, where are you, Kelkar?" Souza asked.

"Still on the island. They sealed the bridge," he replied, though he was aware ferries were up and going.

"Berto's autopsy report is on my desk. The cause of death is heart failure."

"He had a bad heart?"

"Who knows? Anyway, before I forget, they saved your spot on the task force. Return to Goi or miss the bus."

He got that Souza wanted the case wrapped, bow-tied and presented to him soon. But the investigation had not touched bottom yet. Everything else could wait.

"Stop by my office once you get to the capital," Souza urged when he fell silent. "We can talk over a bottle of feni."

Kelkar laughed.

"I'll settle for tea," he said.

"I forgot. Tea for you and something stronger for me," Souza said, his voice on the line lighthearted.

At seven o'clock, Jass unlocked the facility's heavy iron gates. He tipped his slight body forward and moved them to either side and Kelkar steered his mud-streaked car through and stepped out. While Jass gaped, he rolled a gate toward him and climbed up the metal scrollwork and over to the other side.

"Do you lock the gates after hours?" he asked the gardener, pushing the gate into place.

"Yes. But they are also locked when important people visit from Goi," he replied.

"Like whom?"

"People like the Governor of Goi. The big guy was here last week, and his security blocked the gates until he left."

Away in the background, Kelkar noticed a home that emerged from above the treetops.

"Who lives there?" he asked.

"Rish Tilak and his mother, Mira. He has lived there since I began working here a long time ago."

Later, at the front office, a busy Tara paused for a minute when she saw him.

"Naini has run away," she said, sounding rueful.

Chapter 51

Rish watched the moon rise over the hills. A cricket orchestra led by an unseen conductor struck its top notes and paused. Between the song of the insects and the calm, the moon climbed high in the sky with a majestic beauty.

He could hear the soft pad of footsteps from the upper level where his mother lived. They rarely met or talked despite being in such tight quarters, and like ships at night both passed each other and sailed in opposite directions until they crossed paths again.

There was an urgent rapping at the front door, and he got up to check who was outside.

The knocking rung out in the quiet upstairs and broke Mira's sleep. She peeped from across the hallway to see who it could be. Rish answered the door, and she recognized the wraith of a woman in a grungy uniform who shifted from foot to foot on the patio. They whispered in the dark for a while. Mira watched Naini slip in through the door.

"Who is it?" she asked Rish, stepping out of view.

"It is the wind," he said. "Everything is fine."

The quarrel she witnessed earlier occurred between the same employee now in their home and the man found dead. And she had a feeling that the worst was yet to come.

She was still thinking of the night the next morning when there was a low knock on her door.

"You called?" Rish said, and he shut the door behind him.

"I am moving to Goi," she said.

Her remark caught him by surprise because he saw her as more island than mainland. Her visits to Goi were brief, about a day's trip back and forth for meetings with party movers and shakers. And he had assumed she barely tolerated the intrigues in the capital. This decision of hers sounded more like a permanent move.

"You are always welcome here," he said guardedly.

"And what about your plans?" she asked.

The disapproval in her tone transported him to his childhood. To those times when she guessed he was up to nothing good.

"I would like to stay on as director. If that is okay," he said.

"Do as you please," she said with a dash of indifference in her voice.

He stood, hiding his relief.

"There is a detective named Jiva Kelkar on the prowl here. He is investigating the incident. And he may want a word with you and your staff," he said on his way to the door.

"Careful."

"About what?" he said, brushing her off. He slammed the door and left.

A muffled conversation from the lower level of the house had her pause and listen. She let go her breath and reached for her phone.

"Monday," she said to Batti over the phone. "I cleared my calendar."

"Not a moment too soon. He is ready to dig it up," he said.

"Does Tito have the papers?"

"He is on it."

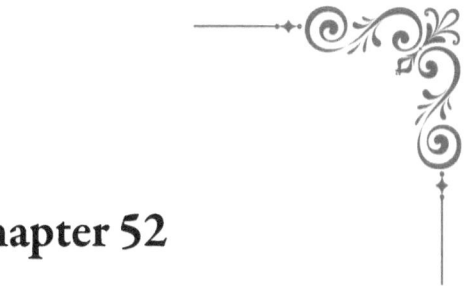

Chapter 52

Bir tried to focus on the picture, but he was having trouble. The ravens dive-bombed him at the studio that morning, and one bird had been angry enough to peck his forehead hard. He felt a stabbing ache build behind his right eye.

"Did you see this person or not, Mr. Munshi?" Kelkar said again, raising his voice up an octave to grab his attention.

"Who is that?" Bir said dully.

"Any suspicious goings on here?"

When Bir shook his head, he scooped up the photograph.

"Wait," Bir said when he had reached the door. "Maybe this is one of those coincidences people talk about. I saw two dead animals within yards of each other."

"It happens in a forest like this. Could be predators. Or kids playing pranks. Contact the front office if you remember something else," he said.

He thought Bir's story was trivial. Then he remembered his rookie case from decades ago. The error he made that time which he aimed never to repeat. And never forget.

On that one occasion, he dismissed a clue at a crime scene, thinking it was unconnected to the events. An experienced senior investigator later picked the clue up and docketed it. It proved to be crucial evidence, and a pivot in the investigation that helped land the department a conviction.

"Show me where you found them," he said, stepping back into the room.

Chapter 53

"He ran into us the other evening on the beach," Claudia said when Kelkar showed them the picture. The couple were the first of the six guests on his list.

"Two guys were roughing him up," Herb said.

"When?" he asked.

"Days before Sandy discovered the body," Herb said, describing the two.

"Did you see what happened?"

"Not really. We left immediately."

"When we came back, there were cops at the location. But not them," she said, closing her hand over Herb's.

"I saw him at the Sizzle the next day," Herb said, unclasping his hand from hers.

She shot a searching glance at him.

"I am sorry, Dee," he said to her, avoiding her gaze. "It has been difficult for me. I lunch at the Sizzle every afternoon."

"I knew it," she breathed. She crossed her arms and stared ahead.

While she stewed, Herb got into details on how hotel staff threw the drunk out. Later that night, out on a walk at the beach, he spotted him yet again.

"And there he was," he continued. "Acting rather funny. I mean, he reminded me so much of an old college buddy who got high on mushrooms. It was eerie."

Chapter 54

"Do you know Naini?" he asked him.
"She does the cleaning here," Rish replied.
"When did you last see her?"
"Previous week."
"Well. Your friend has disappeared," Kelkar said.
"How does this concern me?"
"You had a relationship with her."
"I did not hide it," Rish said, flinching.
"You were not in the open either."
"I do not know where she is," he insisted.
"Are you screwing the help, Mr. Tilak?"
Rish flushed.
"Berto Souza and Naini knew each other. And you know her. He winds up dead. And she goes missing. What say you?" Kelkar said.
"She works here. Like the other employees," Rish replied.
"As innocent as any of them?"
"You are reading too much into it, is what I am saying."
"By the way, aiding a criminal is a serious offense. Think your mother's influence can save you?"
"Keep my mother out of this. It has nothing to do with her."
"Tell her I must interview her too."
Rish reached for his phone.
"I will send her a message," he said.

THE UPTURNING

Kelkar stepped outside and into the daylight. The scent of cut flowers permeated the air. He thought of calendulas in a glass of water on a windowsill. Of an essence still strong inside an empty room.

Chapter 55

"Where are you from?"

Pravesh Doss stuffed his hands deep into his pockets, stifling his urge for a smoke.

"Mumbai," he replied.

"The eyes have it. Soldier?"

"Of a kind."

"A separatist."

"Ex. I write for a living now."

"Not Eelam. Not with that name."

"No."

Kelkar nodded.

"Maoist, then."

"PALM in the northeast."

"They disbanded the Power and Light Movement years ago. Done jail time?"

"Some."

"So, you are a respectable journalist now."

"I try to be."

Kelkar listed his head at the wooded area outside.

"Ever been out there?" he asked.

"Yes, often," Pravesh said.

"You miss all the violence. The murder and mayhem in the Assam jungles."

"Not at all."

"Did you go recently?"

He paused. It was a long enough pause for Kelkar to stare up from his notes.

"You saw something," he said.

"Yes, I did."

The admission had slipped out of him, and he appeared none too happy with himself.

"Do you remember when?" Kelkar asked.

"It was a Wednesday, a day before police identified the body."

"What did you see?"

"I heard metal strike a rock, roughly fifty yards to my left. A man was there, in the embankment below."

Pravesh described him as being gaunt, with knotty hair.

"Let's check it out. Shall we?" Kelkar said, walking out.

They went in the brook's direction, with him steps behind Pravesh who came to an abrupt stop. A lone boulder wedged between the trees rested twenty yards away from the death scene. Trees still had yellow police tape tied at their trunks. The snapped off ends of the tape trailed along the forest floor.

"Life in the jungle sharpened my hearing. I have good ears. A metallic object hit that rock you see between the trees. I am sure of it."

Kelkar pushed the tape aside. He poked at the soft vegetation that encircled the stone but detected nothing. Crime branch squad had scoured the section with a fine toothcomb, no doubt.

"And where was the man?"

When Pravesh pointed toward the death site, he felt his excitement mount. Here was an eyewitness who observed a man mucking about where Berto Souza lay dead. The case had taken another fortuitous turn.

Chapter 56

The year 1975 was a page in the book of his life Kelkar remembered word for word. Indira Gandhi, the prime minister of India, declared an Emergency that year with a sweeping decree. A decree meant to curb 'internal disturbances' and give her sole control of the nation. It was a time when an innocent comment blurted offhand could result in a decade or more in jail. Fear choked people, pounded out the joys of life.

The word itself had a pressing quality, and he felt the heft of it even though he was a mere boy during that dark interlude. It felt as if the world he knew was ending. The end brought about by the power-mad ringleaders of a mob.

His father, a senior state official in those days, loved to have friends over on weekends for a drink. They never missed a single weekend. The close-knit group debated everything under the sun, but what riled them most was the current state of affairs in the country. They argued the government's injustices, their fiery talk fueled by large pegs of smuggled whisky.

The door stood open while the adults had discussed the growing power of the police and army. And he remembered standing outside, afraid for his opinionated father, and gripped by a concern the authorities would show up and whisk him and his companions to jail. Loose lips got you in a lot of trouble that year, and every utterance was worth a hundred times its weight.

THE UPTURNING

The grave risk of physical and mental torture did not stop protest movements in the nation. In Goi, the leader of the revolt who marched with activists was Mira Tilak. The image of her flashing eyes and windswept hair had stayed with him. And when he thought of her, those troubling Emergency memories resurfaced.

Translucent drapes drawn across the bow windows cast a cool shade over the room. The lazy dust motes stirred by a ceiling fan lifted in a languid dance between them. She waved him to a chair by the window. He was still tangled up in his idea of her, and he glanced away to prevent himself from staring.

"Are you related to Yash Kelkar?" she asked, taking a seat near him.

She was referring to his grandfather. He was a respected civil rights advocate in British India who worked for the nation after independence. It was an era all but forgotten. The country, with sights locked on the future, had outgrown its oppressive past.

"My grandfather," he said, surprised for a moment.

"I noticed a resemblance."

"A compliment," he said with a smile.

"He was a brilliant lawyer. A patriot, and a great man," she said.

"Your thoughts on the Souza case."

"What does the autopsy report say?"

"Death caused by congestive heart failure with secondary complications."

"You sound like a skeptic, though."

"There could be more to it."

She made light of her meeting with Souza and called it routine. A candid chat among old friends, she said. Nothing more. An awkward pause stretched, and then she spoke up first.

"Are you looking for a young woman?" she said.

"Yes. We think the victim followed her to the island," he said.

"Is she a suspect?"

"I am investigating the possibility."

"Last week, I witnessed an altercation from my window. It happened between a worker and a scruffy character who does not belong here. The two of them exchanged words. When he pulled at her arm, she fought back and shoved him hard. He fell, while she flew off running."

She reached for a pair of pocket binoculars at her desk.

"These are useful as one grows older. I got a clear view from here," she said.

He held up the photograph.

"Was this the person?" he asked.

After a quick study of the picture, she said he was.

"Do you like flowers, detective?" she said to him, changing tack.

"I appreciate them," he replied.

"An island superstition tells of certain flowers that are best left outdoors. If you bring them into the home, you bring in terrible luck."

"I am not one for superstitions. They do little good to the believer."

"Island lore has gotten to me. That's all I can say."

Her eyes flashed with humor, and the irony in them had him smiling at her. He understood her obliqueness, her reasons for being vague. And as he raced down the stairs, he called Rego.

"Arrange for surveillance on the Tilak house. Start at once. I have a suspicion Naini is hiding here," he said to him.

Chapter 57

A muddle of stuff spilled out from an open suitcase on the floor. Vikki moved things aside and cleared a way through the room.

"Seen anything unusual here?" Kelkar asked her.

"To be honest, yes," she said. "Strange things have happened. But no worries overall. It has been beautiful here, I must say."

"What strange things?"

"I got lost at a party. While I was searching for the exit, I saw a man with metal teeth beating somebody. There was some crazy yelling and screaming going on. A second man standing close by acted like a sentry of sorts. Like he was his goon or something. The entire episode spooked me because I recognized one of them. I noticed him on the shore earlier."

"Who is he?"

"I don't know. He walks about the island. Thin, very odd in appearance, and with his hair tangled about his shoulders. Kinda streaky beige hair. Sorta like dry sand. He had a woman with him all the time. The one who washed up on the coast, you know. That day Sandy and I were at the spa when everybody went nuts. We ran out with the others. And it was her, lying there dead."

"Sabine Parker. Her name."

She rubbed at her elbows, close to tears.

"Pretty name for a pretty girl. To be honest, all this death here gives me bad vibes. I try not to think about it," she said.

On his path to the door, he saw the Cimmerian headdress near the rest of her stuff. She held it for him while he took a picture.

Chapter 58

"What did you get?" Kelkar asked. He took the tiger prawn by its tail and had a bite.

They were at the Temperado that weekend eating lunch. With the food came glasses of a syrupy raw mango drink.

"I heard Lala bought a huge stretch of land near Souza's estate," Rego said.

"So you said. How big?"

"10,000 acres."

"That much?"

"I had my doubts it was him."

"And so?"

"A friend in the state clerk's office did me a favor. He pulled up recent real estate records."

"Lala is not the buyer."

"No."

"What about the jewelry store?"

"He did buy the store, but not the land."

"Who bought the land?"

"No idea, yet. The fine print disguises the owner's identity, so I followed the paper trail and dug around. A company representing the owner purchased land worth over a thousand crores this month. And that company is owned by MV Foundation, a private entity."

"Could be a front."

"A setup that shrouds their dealings in anonymity."

"How convenient for them."

"I checked. It is all legal."

"Is there an owner on record?"

"They are persons unknown. With assets being held in trust by a nominee."

"Who is the nominee?"

"A local lawyer by the name of Sid Tito. Now, this is even more interesting. He was a former attorney at Vishal Batti's law firm."

"Hah."

"He runs the HRD when he is not lawyering."

"The herd?"

"History Reclamation Department."

"A hog of a bureaucracy."

"They have a bad habit of taking over private land under some pretext and auctioning it to the highest bidder."

"Poke deeper. This is a power-hungry hog with a thick hide."

Rego nodded.

"What did Tito have to say?"

"He claims he left Batti's enterprise a year ago and is on his own. I leaned on him, but he didn't give. He won't talk."

"Did you interview Souza's driver?"

"I saved the best for last. Veliz borrowed the state sedan on Wednesday for some business in Pavim."

"Has he done that before?"

"Never. He claimed it was on Souza's behalf. The driver said it relieved him when he returned the car in one piece. Veliz is terrible on the road."

"Souza know of this?"

"He knows. But he trusts Veliz."

"And does he call for a cab to attend state affairs?"

"Souza is campaigning up north these days. He travels in an ordinary Monitor when he visits dirt poor constituencies. Makes for better optics and all that."

"I have interviews to conduct here. While I am at it, tail two drug dealers for me."

He described the daily routine of Sec and Thak. And of his suspicions of a nexus among them and Fereira.

Rego signaled for the check.

"No dessert?" Kelkar asked, looking askance at him. He was aware of the deputy's sweet tooth.

"I thought you might be in a hurry, sir," Rego said.

Kelkar skipped to the menu's dessert section.

"The bebintia any good?" he asked.

"It is the island's best."

"Bebintia sounds like someone's nosy aunt. Not delectable at all."

"Quite the opposite, in fact."

"What do we have here?"

Kelkar read off the menu.

"An amazing confection made with fresh egg yolks, butter, and forest honey, the menu says."

"Fifty egg yolks."

"Fifty, eh?"

"It is the Governor's favorite dessert."

"The bebintia it is, then."

Rego broke into a lopsided grin. He waved at the waiter and ordered dessert.

Chapter 59

They were in the recreation room in the middle of a carrom game. Vikki practiced a thumb flip with the striker which skated an inch and went nowhere. Greg won easily, sliding his last piece into the pocket and claiming victory. When he stepped in, they broke the game. He began with some general questions.

"Well," Greg said. "A speeding car almost hit me in Nerul."

"I got a shot of his rear plates," Vikki said, jumping up and handing her phone to Kelkar.

"It careened by waaay too fast if you ask me. And that flag hoisted up front looked legit, like a politician's car."

"That is the Governor's official car," Kelkar replied.

"See, I was right!" she exclaimed.

"No kidding. It was at the north entrance last week. They blocked the gates and all," Greg said.

Kelkar scrutinized the images. The tinted glass obscured the Spaar's interior and the driver's identity. Did Souza drive to Bolim on Wednesday, two days after he visited Mira Tilak? His instincts said no. His entourage was nowhere in sight. And no official at his level traveled without one. Perhaps this is what Rego had reported earlier.

Greg set carrom pieces on the powdered board. He dusted his hands and aimed, and the pieces scattered. He passed the striker to Vikki for her turn.

"Get the queen," Kelkar said to her.

THE UPTURNING

She targeted the fuchsia queen but missed the shot and dropped one of his pieces instead. Exasperated, she slid the striker back to him.

Chapter 60

The power went out at 4 am and the air conditioner coughed and wound to a halt. He glanced at his watch. It was much too early. The closed room ran out of air, and he tossed and turned and woke up. He lifted the sheets off him and swung his legs over the side. A cool salty wind from the cay blew inside when he flung open the window. The birds grew more assertive, chirping louder by the minute as a sliver of sun rose in the eastern skies.

He set the electric kettle on for his first dose of tea. At the desk, he slid the plastic wrapping off the cash bundle and counted the notes. They amounted to forty thousand US dollars, a valued currency among drug dealers on the island. He sorted them by denomination and clicked pictures of the serial numbers. Then he backed up the information in his notepad.

The kettle whistled and he made the tea. He was at the window when he noticed that the birds had stopped their chatter. There was something peculiar about the quiet, and he waited to hear a screech or a squawk but there was not a peep from them. This silence from birds who talked and warbled every morning got him wondering if there was another earthquake coming. Or maybe rain. He read somewhere that birds did that. Went quiet when the weather was going to change. He looked down.

From the street below, familiar sounds of people he heard daily drifted through. A bicyclist on his paper route passed by, ringing his bell. He could hear the gleeful *ha ha ha ha* from a laughter yoga class in the park across. And the muffled jazz riffs playing from the room next door.

He tilted an ear to the outdoors and reached for his service weapon in reflex. Outside the window, the leaves on trees rippled in waves that rolled from one to the other. It was a high sea of green. He stared at their tops until his eyes burned.

The chirrups picked up again. Tiny sparrows and finches flew in and out the bushes hunting for a worm or a tasty bug to eat. He eased up. It was likely nothing.

He resumed his reading, noting that the morgue completed the autopsy two hours after receipt of the body. The forensic pathologist followed standard procedures. X-rays, blood, and tissue samples showed congested organs, which was typical of a heart attack victim in the last stages of life. The toxicology screen results proved negative with organs and blood indicating no remnants of poison.

Berto's heart ceased beating the day of his death. He wanted to know why.

He swallowed the lukewarm dregs from his cup. The medical examiner's office opened at eight, and he had questions for Dr. Sahu.

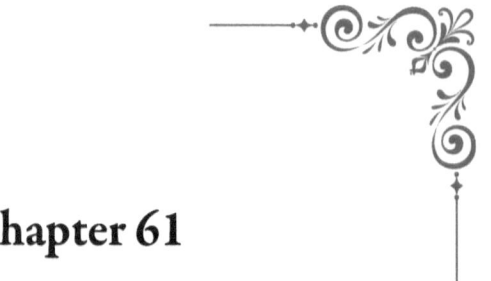

Chapter 61

Tourists crowded this particular section of the waterfront, a popular place for people-watching. The atmosphere was livelier here, with cheap food stalls, souvenir shops and discount clothing stores hemming a wide boulevard. Away from the busyness, at the rocky shoreline where ocean met land, tide pools with barnacles, fish, tadpoles, and marine grass, reflected the blue skies. Music blared. Kids splashed. Parents scolded. Pets rampaged. Hawkers peddled their wares.

It was a perfect day to be at the beach. Rego lay on a recliner in the umbrella's shade, looking like a tourist enjoying the view. Though he was not much of a reader, he held an open novel as a prop which served his purpose. He tried hard to look engrossed by the contents. Now and then, when the printed words swam before his eyes, he took a break and checked out the scenery.

Two men to the right of him moseyed his way, and their affected casualness had his guard up. He slid his hat down his brow and watched them through the fabric's weave.

Rego followed Sec and Thak to a café, and he grabbed a far table from where he could see the pair. Soon a cop in uniform joined them. The three chatted, hunched over their drinks.

When the suspects left, Fereira sat alone and nursed a glass of feni. Rego ordered a beer from the bar, and he moved to the table next to him.

"Cheers!" he said, lifting his drink at Fereira.

Rego had his attention right away. Fereira gulped his drink in a single shot and set his glass down with a thud.

"Goi police?" he asked Rego.

"On assignment," Rego said.

"You work for that jerk Kelkar?" he said.

"Regrettably, I do. But you didn't hear it from me," Rego said.

"I told him this is a straightforward case. Berto Souza died of heart failure, plain and simple."

"It may not be that plain and simple."

"Okay. I will grant you that. But he is interfering in our affairs."

"How so?"

"He is snooping around on the island. What for? We can do the job."

"So you guys have an investigation on?"

"Yes and no. He was the Governor's brother, so we must go through some formalities. Keeping up appearances and all that."

"We heard Berto got mixed up in a dirty drug deal. He hid big cash that dealers never found," he said, keeping it down.

"What money are you talking about?" Fereira asked.

His jaw dropped wide in comical surprise and Rego had to repress a laugh.

"Kelkar is in Bolim hunting for the buried cash."

"That's crap!"

"Then he sent me on a wild goose chase after two drug dealers. Between you and me, it was a complete waste of time."

As they spoke, his phone pinged. Rego shook his head, chuckling at the text on the screen.

"Now he says he will resume his search tomorrow. What a madman, I tell you."

A flustered Fereira shambled out of his chair, his phone glued to his ear. He plodded down the beach with his arms up in an animated conversation with the person at the other end. Rego drained his beer over the sand. That was easy, too easy. Fereira could not see beyond his own nose. He gave Kelkar a call and updated him.

Chapter 62

"Almost done here," the doctor said, his face angled over a microscope. He switched through a series of specimens and tagged the slides. Then he wheeled his chair over.

"What's this about?" he said.

"The Souza autopsy report," Kelkar replied.

"The report is accurate," he said stiffly.

"Sure."

"Sure?"

"I have some concerns about it."

"I do not. And neither should you."

It was an unwieldy start, and Kelkar backpedaled quickly. He talked frankly of his suspicions and the doctor began warming up to him.

"You see, we go by the autopsy findings. And reconstruct events from what is in there. The ME's office does not do investigations," the doctor said.

"That is the job of the police department."

"Which in this case was derelict in its duty."

"The island police reek."

"Aptly put, detective," the doctor said. "And so based on what we had, I concluded my report and gave it to police."

"The manner of death was undetermined. Why?"

"A relevant question."

"He died of congestive heart failure."

"It caused his heart to quit, yes. That's the what. But I detected no signs of heart disease."

"So you are saying the how or why - the manner - is unknown."

"Yes, the evidence on hand is inconclusive."

"And new evidence could change that."

"A rare thing, but it happens."

"You mean you had your doubts, too?" he said to the doctor.

"Everybody involved in the case wanted the autopsy finished at top speed. Bolim police dragged their feet. They were reluctant to investigate and uncover the truth. Those incidents had my antennae up and twitchy," the doctor said.

"Are you the island's only pathologist?"

"I am. But a coroner north of the island also conducts dissections. He was eager to autopsy Mr. Souza even though this is not his jurisdiction. Maybe Goi pressured him, or perhaps it was not that at all."

"Did police begin an investigation?"

"Far from it. I am guessing you met Officer Savio Fereira?"

"I have had the pleasure."

"He declared it an open and shut case. Unbelievable!" the doctor said. "Later, Peter Souza contacted me about the postmortem findings. He demanded I wrap up before the upcoming elections. I consider an autopsy report an instrument of closure, yet here we are."

He laid out photographs in rows on a table.

"This is what we have," he said. "At least two individuals were present near the body before a guest discovered him dead. One or both of those individuals rifled through his front and back trouser pockets."

"They are turned inside out. I see that."

"He was faced belly down at livor mortis stage when purplish blood pools in the extremities because of gravity. Here is the unmistakable blenching effect of a branch pressing into the stomach and doing the opposite. The branch forced blood into the insides. And here, you see this mark on his back?

"The body was flipped over."

"Right. The same thick bough marked his spinal column."

"A witness saw a man named Sec at the death scene."

"Is Sec a Kori?"

"No. He is a tourist drug dealer of sorts from overseas."

"It is possible he handled the corpse, but unlikely he killed Berto Souza."

"I do not follow," he said. This changed the trajectory of his thinking.

"I'll get to it in a minute," the doctor said. "When I cut the anterior side clear, I smelled bitter almonds in all body orifices and cavities. That particular smell had me suspect cyanide. But tests turned up negative for it. Major organs were all bloated, which is typical of cardiac arrest. His heart stopped beating, killing him."

"Why is that?"

"I could not tell why."

"Any latent fingerprints recovered?"

"None. Surface decomposition was severe. However, a mud patch a few feet off tells a unique story."

The doctor held up a picture. It showed an indentation, with sole prints leading away from the spot. Petals fixed to a hairpin and bits of glass lay nearby.

"A second person, a woman, approximated the site sometime after he expired," he said. "My guess is she fell and created that cavity you see in this picture here. Her bangles splintered during the fall. And a flower and hairpin fastened to her hair dropped. I doubt she came anywhere close to the body. In fact, she ran from it."

Dr. Sahu excused himself. When he returned, an acerbic scent came with him.

"Have you heard about Kori curers, detective?" he said.

"I learned curers bred on poison lived here ages ago."

"That was then. The virulent ones of old are gone, but there exist powerful curers today who settle disputes with a deadly toxin borrowed from nature. Another breed of medicine man, with an equivalent malignancy."

"What kind of toxin?"

"A toxin from a wild vine called *datura sattivus*, a subspecies of the datura family, and indigenous to Fins Island. The berries contain atropine – a potent tropane alkaloid. A poison more destructive than any other datura variety."

"What's with the eyes?"

The cadaver's eye sockets had withdrawn into the skull. Paper thin patches of skin covered the hollows.

"Collapsed sockets are an extraordinary symptom of *d. sattivus* poisoning. The alkaloid in atropine is an anticholinergic. Substances that block a heart's normal functions."

"How?"

"They overstimulate the heart and cause erratic patterns. The heart races, ratcheting up the pressure in the skull. The pressure ruptures the eyeballs."

"Like a version of belladonna?"

"A deadlier version. With a million times more toxicity. It is the only datura subspecies to leave no trace in a victim's body. Certain provocative indications linger after."

"Like?"

"The bitter almond smell, the ruptured eyeballs. And weird conduct right before death. I am optimistic science will catch up one day."

Kelkar described Berto's quirky behavior in the days before he died.

"Those are atropine toxicity symptoms," the doctor said.

"You mean the delirium, hallucinations, and phobias?"

"Yes. That occurs when the poison enters the bloodstream. But other crucial clues are absent."

"Such as?"

"After the victim dies, the curer slaughters two animals in a ritual and places them near the deceased. Our investigator found none. Throws the theory up in the air."

"We got a tip on mutilated animals about half a mile from the scene. I took pictures," he said, showing the doctor the images.

"Oh yes, just as I imagined," he said. He swiped at them, getting worked up.

"See that powdery blue substance on them?" Kelkar asked.

"Salt. The curer lives in Kori Cave. A cave of blue salt. Another significant clue."

"Could have been someone else."

"It is the curer who makes the fatal cut. No other tribal is allowed to."

"Why kill animals?"

"The animals are otherworldly companions for victims after their spirit exits the body. Outlandish as it may be, a curer believes in compassion for the dead even though he is the slayer."

"And who is a standard victim?"

"In most cases, they are tribals. Families claim the bodies and do not report it."

"So circumstantial evidence we have points to a curer."

"True, but impossible to verify since *d. sattivus* is a murder weapon that vanishes. Anyway, curers do not administer the poison themselves. They pick an ordinary tribal who can mingle among people for the task. But it is he, the ghost, who stalks the poisoned. He waits, and once they succumb he etches his mark. Like this one here," the doctor said, indicating the scar under Berto's jaw.

"That scar baffled me at the identification."

"The design is a representation of a *d. sattivus* vine. Analogous to a signature if you will. Made with a knife's tip."

"A message that the curer is responsible for death."

"Yes."

"And those blue crystals in the cut? Salt, again?"

"Salt in the wound. Yes."

"What sort of blade does that?"

"Two forged weapons the Kori use are daggers. One, a *katar* or scorpion dagger, which has two undulating lethal blades. The second is a smaller *nakha*. Shaped like a tiger's claw with a lower handle."

"The cut's curved line appears more like a *nakha's* work. Shorter handle and blade allow for more precision."

"I concur."

"Have you autopsied any others?"

Dr. Sahu wheeled his chair over to a cabinet and got a photograph from a slim folder in the drawer.

"One. This is a picture of a believed poisoning death from a decade ago," he said.

Leaf lines akin to the one below Berto's chin etched the face of a man in the picture.

"Who was he?"

"A John Doe. All his organs displayed extreme congestion signs. Atypical for someone so young. Atropine's half-life is an hour, and this victim had been dead twenty-four hours when we located him. The Kori stole the body one night and ransacked the entire lab. I had taken these pictures home to find answers, but the rest is all gone."

"How do you think they gave the poison to Berto?"

"It could have been slipped into his drink. The substance is tasteless and odorless. He probably did not know. I am confident this is a tribal killing.

"Which is why this Sec chap cannot be the killer."

"He tampered with the body later. Further, there was no notable physical trauma inflicted on Berto. None of his cuts and bruises were serious enough to lead to his death."

The doctor handed him a key chain with a Spoker centavo attached at its end.

"We located this by a boulder near the dead man. It may help your investigation," he said, closing the file.

"One last question. How did Sabine Parker die?"

"Officially, she drowned."

"What's your take?"

"She had all the marks of a death by strangulation, but it was a tough hypothesis to corroborate."

"Why is that?"

"Because the body was in deep waters for days. And had decomposed to a considerable degree."

Dr. Sahu began to stuff the photographs into a folder with quivering hands.

"You have a drinking problem, doctor," Kelkar said to him.

"Not sure what you mean," the doctor replied.

"You would make a terrible expert on the stand. They will rip you apart."

"I want to crack this case as much as you do, detective. This is important to me."

The doctor swiveled on his chair and went back to his lab instruments, ending their conversation.

Chapter 63

Kelkar set the photograph on the coffee table. Sandy shifted in her seat and gave the picture a quick peek.

"No... he looked...it... he was different."

"Dead, you mean?"

She shook her head and worked her mouth, still distressed by the memory.

"Did you run into a thin man and a woman on the beach?" he asked her.

"That dreadful man! He said the most awful stuff to her," she said.

"What did he say?"

"She dropped the bag she was lugging, and he began to yell at her. 'I could strangle you now,' he said.

"Those were his exact words?"

"Those were his exact words. They claim she drowned, but who is to say he did not finish her first?"

"Why were you out in the woods?"

"I watch birds."

"A birdwatcher."

"An avid one."

"And what does a birdwatcher do around here?"

"She wanders about the wilderness, verifies sightings and takes tons of pictures."

"What kind of bird wears this?" he asked, handing her the feather from his pocket.

"An Orbed Salten does!" she gasped with surprise.

"The Salten is an extinct bird."

"Right, defunct since 1901. I saw one, or rather I saw the tail feathers of a Salten pop above the bushes one day. Quite puzzling because the bird was a cave-dweller. But I know what I saw."

"And I plucked that same nonexistent bird's feather out of a tree."

She laughed.

"It appears you did," she said.

She lifted the feather high. As she waved it in the air, the silky fronds fell, and the tiny ornamental orbs at their ends glowed with a flicker of blue light.

"Watch," she said to him. "It is magic."

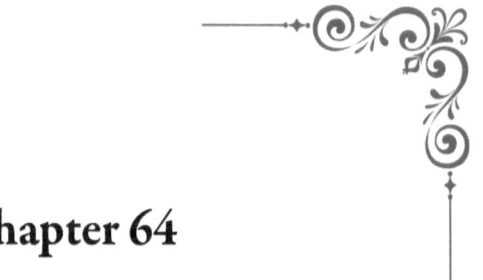

Chapter 64

The trees at the grove were like the stout legs of ogres at a gathering. Dry brush grew below the tree trunks, giving derelicts a furtive refuge at sundown. Litter from bottles, plastic bags and metal cans in bubblegum colors poked out from the seaweed that carpeted the ground.

In the brush, Rego found a couple with vacuous eyes getting high off a glue can. The dreary duo fought between sniffs, while their hungry children crawled around eating dirt for food. They cleared the family out and onward to the open sands and set up watch behind the trees.

An hour after, the drug peddling drifters trudged across to the grove's boundary. Sec who was ahead limped in followed by a jumpy Thak.

When he saw them Sec backed off and sat down.

"Where are you from?" Kelkar asked Sec.

"He is from Spoker Island," Thak said.

An angry Sec lunged at him because he spoke out and Rego pushed them apart.

"You answer this time. Where are you from?" he repeated, pointing at Sec.

"Spoker Island," he said.

"What kind of visa?"

"Tourist."

"Who do you work for?"

"Tinnu Chacha. We work for him."

"See, that was easy. It is illegal to work on a tourist visa. I should haul you to jail this minute and let you rot there. Your embassy gives a damn about trash like you, anyway."

Sec hung his head in a tetchy silence.

"We got your key chain at the scene. Pretty damning evidence to me," Kelkar said.

"You can be charged with suspected murder," Rego said.

"I went looking for my money. He was already dead," a surly Sec said to them.

"And you! Where are you from?" Kelkar said to Thak.

"Larabos Island," Thak replied.

"You are a hardworking drug dealer, I assume?"

"I am a student here."

"There is no university on the island."

"Please, I don't want any trouble. Sec is not lying. He told me a man flew through the trees as he was searching the body. Tell them, Sec."

They spun around at a snapping sound and watched Fereira clomp over the woody scrub and rush into the clearing.

"Here comes misery," Rego said to Kelkar.

Fereira said nothing to them, but his face swelled with spite.

"Those two are suspects in the case. Keep them in jail," Kelkar said.

Fereira cuffed the men and led them away.

"And watch out for their uncle," Rego shouted, laughing.

In the car, they took a break. Rego returned calls, and he caught up with his mail. He deleted the infinite scroll of spam and the unnecessary stuff from his inbox. The resulting blank space satisfied him, temporary though it was.

They were on their way to a nearby café when his phone beeped with a text from the Sizzle owner. The message said Sal worked for a diving company in neighboring Dona Marina, a town five miles north of Bolim. They made an abrupt U-turn and drove out to the marina.

Wood cutouts of bright blue waves and fish in flight lined the reed walls of the shack. Puffer fish and pygmy sharks with filmy eyes dangled from fishing rods propped at the door. Far out on the spangled sea in front of the shack, a white catamaran with tourists on board bobbed in the cobalt waters. A nimble man on the boat darted from deck to deck with wetsuits, helping the passengers strap and belt oxygen tanks.

Kelkar rapped at the shack's open door. Inside, a thickset man lounged by a pile of surfboards, joking with a teenage boy. He approached them and said he was Jude Mascarenha, the owner of the joint.

"I can give you two-for-one scuba dive deal today. Best on the beach," he said.

"Does a Sal Bilbao work for you?" Kelkar asked.

"Why do you ask?" he said. His gap-toothed smile evaporated a little.

Kelkar flashed his badge.

"Goi police investigating a death in Bolim. We need a word with him," he said.

"*Borem.* Okay," Mascarenha said.

He came out and waved his arms at the catamaran. The sunburnt man on board dived in and swam to the shallows. He waded through the water and ran toward them.

"Sal *khoi assa* Johnny? Johnny, where is Sal?" he said to him as he got closer.

"He dashed off minutes earlier. And I have a boatload of customers waiting to start the dive," the man named Johnny complained.

"Ay, Mario! *Modot kor* out on the boat. Go help Johnny with the boat. I will manage here," Mascarenha said, giving instructions to the teen. "It is impossible to find decent workers. The island has gone to the dogs."

"Where did Sal go?" Kelkar asked Johnny.

"Back to his home," he said.

"That one has a screw loose up there," Mascarenha said, twirling his fingers in circles at his temples. "He began two days ago but consider him fired by me. These Kori are a major nuisance. The government gives them employment, gives them special status, but they do not stay long at any job. Businesses here are all reluctant to hire them."

"Hold on a minute. Sal is a Kori?"

"Oh yes. He is from Pavim. You should have no problem finding him. Had his ears and nose tip chewed as a wee boy when a jackal dragged him into the forest. Good luck smoking him out, though. Kori will act deaf, dumb, and blind to protect their own."

They finished the session and walked to the sand-washed parking lot.

"The plot's as thick as aspic," he said, buckling his seatbelt.

"But tasty," Rego said.

He pulled out the lot and picked up the highway that led to Pavim.

"We have no vehicular access after a point. Our last leg must be on foot through the forest," Rego said, poring over a map on his phone.

"A trek sharpens the mind. And bring the flashlights with you. No sense in us straying off the trail at night."

Chapter 65

They hiked down the slope and through the dell. In a broad mud-tamped clearing Kori in ceremonial dress danced with their forearms at each other's waists. The couples grouped together in pairs and sang as they danced, and their stomping feet sent an undercurrent all the way to the rear of the tall brushwood where they now hid.

At the clearing's edges, an iron cauldron simmered on a wood fire. A bent elder stood on an elevated stand and stirred the contents with a ladle, blending the potion in slow circles. He stepped down often to poke and feed the flames with dry branches, and the sparks from burning wood ash floated across the meadow.

The revelry ended for a break; the lilts of music waned and became fainter. While women shifted to the corners, the men moved forward and sat in rows near the fire. The elder poured a liquid from the pot into small gourd cups, and he went around giving the seated group the drinks. In time, they appeared intoxicated, their jaws slack and loose.

The revels resumed, and the music increased pace and swelled to a crescendo. At its peak, the elder lifted his arm in a sign and movement and song ceased. The tribe gazed at the treetops, eyes glinting with anticipation, and rocked shoulder-to-shoulder with a restrained hum. Through a breach in the brushwood, they saw the crowd's focus directed upwards, and Kelkar and Rego felt an instinctive reptilian gripping at the scruff of their necks. Their attention swiveled from the waiting tribals and back again to the black trees.

The tree shadows morphed into the moving shape of a man who slithered down with a leopard's litheness. A short dagger, curved like a talon, dangled in a sleeve at the side of his waist. His face was shielded with a magnificent warmask of feathers that fanned in an arc above his head. As he moved the fronds dipped and changed tones, and the orbed tips scintillated in the firelight. It was as if a timeless Kori curer had been resuscitated from an archaic photograph and returned to life in color.

After many rounds of dancing, the curer stopped. The elder walked to him and offered him a filled gourd cup which he emptied in a single draft. He drank from the cup, replenished three times by the elder, then climbed up a tree with agile ease and disappeared. Under the trees, the inebriated dropped like gnats and one by one the women and elders left the scene.

They tested their legs, cramped after the long watch, and advanced to the men sprawled over each other.

At Bolim police station, the fresh-faced officer came away from his post and began recording the information they supplied.

Kelkar rubbed his gritty eyes. They had been up all night.

"Lock him up," he said, pointing to Sal.

The officer picked his pen from the page and hesitated.

"What's the charge?" he asked.

"Disturbing the peace. And he may have played a part in the Berto Souza case."

The air-rending wail of fire trucks drowned out the conversation, and he waited until the blasts faded and he recovered his hearing. At least a dozen trucks had driven by; a large number for a modest town like Bolim.

"Where is the fire?" he asked the officer.

"At the ME's building downtown. The entire place is ablaze from the reports we received. All our officers were dispatched there."

"Stay here and keep on top of things, Rego," he said to his befuddled deputy who was sorting the paperwork the officer handed him.

The sirens resound launched a shot of adrenaline through Kelkar. He sprinted up to the attendant at the door, swiped the keys to a patrol car from his desk and drove off.

Chapter 66

H e followed the fire trucks heading downtown through rush hour. Every lane was clogged with distracted drivers intent on getting home. On the far side of the traffic, gray miasma over the rooftops blotted the sky, and he braced for the coming sight. He cut across lanes and exited the logjam of traffic, parked a block from the business district, and then rushed the distance on foot.

At the building's front, firefighters on ladders fought the eruption, their clenched faces smeared with falling ash and dirt. He could see the fire burned the fiercest in the records department at the upper reaches of the building. A flash shattered the windows, and fragments cascaded to the ground in a shining fall of rain. From there the flares leaped up the roof, and in minutes torched tiles broke and popped like corn kernels in a hot skillet.

A dry wind drove the heated air toward him, and he tore the opposite way and made a detour to escape. At the end of the driveway, employees in white lab coats stood by a group of emergency personnel rendering first aid, and he asked one of them what was going on. A staffer said it could be arson, but everybody in the affected area was evacuated and safe. The news relieved him, and he checked the crowds to see if Dr. Sahu was anywhere around.

He got sight of him on a parallel sidewalk, and he crossed the street to him. Soot streaked his skin and wiry hair. Airborne embers had burned tiny holes in his clothes. They stared at the blaze together, fascinated despite themselves. It was flames, smoke, and water everywhere they looked. Years of his research lay on the shelves and inside cabinets of the building, he told Kelkar. And he doubted whether any of it would survive the fire.

"I saved you this," he said, thrusting a smoke-stained folder at him.

"What happened last night?" Kelkar asked.

"Lab workers left at about nine in the evening," he said, clearing his throat. "And I had the entire lab to myself, which I welcomed. Anyway, the windows were open that warm night when a cold shudder crept up my spine."

"Strange. One early morning at the lodge, I had gooseflesh for no good reason."

"It was unnerving. I thought my mind played a trick. That perhaps being alone in a vacant room had made me oversensitive. I put the thought aside and I got involved in an experiment for a couple of hours. It was quiet and I liked it. Then at one in the morning, mongrels began to howl in the street below. The dogs often hang by the lab, barking at the slightest noise. I tried feeding them treats, but it was no use. They raced toward those trees beyond and returned mewling, their tails down. I was closing the windows shut when a shadow moved past the trees. It all but vanished before I grasped its nature."

The doctor spaced out for several moments. Kelkar noticed his expression change.

"The shadow you saw. Were you -" he said and stopped.

"I have been sober since we last talked," the doctor said.

"Any guesses?"

"The Kori. Remember what took place with our John Doe from ages ago?"

"Sure."

"They could not get the body this time. It was shipped to Goi yesterday."

"Where did the fire start?"

"Records. We store case files at the end of a workday there."

THE UPTURNING

"Coincidences make me suspicious."
"And what are the odds of that here, detective?"

Chapter 67

Fereira stood outside the station waving his arms at Rego, clearly agitated by something. He complained the cells were packed beyond capacity, and he insisted Sal Bilbao did not belong in his prison. His fussy irritation puzzled Rego who pointed out the case spanned both regions. Sal was in 'his' jail because they discovered the victim on the island. But Fereira would hear none of it, and he carried on with his rant.

"This is the island. Not Goi. You have no authority here. Why is your prisoner in my jail?" he said.

"The victim died here, so why not?" Rego protested.

An adamant Fereira yelled he wanted them out of his precinct.

"They have shipped Berto Souza to Goi."

"And?"

"Take your witness and interrogate him there. I am not responsible for him anymore."

They argued until Kelkar showed up and inquired what the problem was.

"Missed your morning glass of feni, Fereira?" he joked, flashing a grin at Rego.

"Collect your junk and leave the island," Fereira said.

He paced in circles, thinking of ways to make it more difficult for them.

"Release Sal to our custody. I will note the lack of cooperation from island police officers. Your station in particular," Kelkar said.

"You ought to return to the mainland and stop this idiocy. Souza does not care about the case," Fereira said.

His piggish face turned sinister as he said that, and his nostrils flared with resentment.

Kelkar wheeled on his heels.

"Did he say that to you?" he demanded angrily.

Fereira sidled aside. He held his hands up in a gesture to show he was only the messenger.

"I picked up rumors that blew here," he said.

"What rumors?"

"They transported the body straight from airport to crematorium. No proper burial or anything. And no sign of the Governor anywhere. People in the know in Goi claim he wants no details in the press. When you put two and two together, it makes you wonder."

A furious Kelkar pulled out of the station.

He slowed when he glimpsed the sea through swaying coastal trees, and he parked off ramp for a breather.

"If what Fereira says is correct -" Rego said, when they stepped out of the car.

"He is a rotten liar. Vermin like him lie for a livelihood," he said still angry.

He cut him off, but with a dawning sense he could be right.

"But if what he heard is true?" Rego repeated.

He considered the possibility. That Fereira, insufferable as he was, may have a point.

"It means Souza is either spinning a web or is trapped in one," he admitted.

"What do we do with Sal here?"

"Let's get him talking. Make certain he is on record."

Kelkar grabbed a water bottle from the cup holder in the car.

"Talk, Sal," he said to him.

"Some water," Sal said, pointing his chin at the bottle. His words were chopped into bits by his thirst.

Kelkar took a slow, deep swig of water and tossed the bottle back into the vehicle.

"We are on route to Goi," he said.

"I won't go to the mainland," Sal said.

"Then tell us what happened."

"I was to slip the powder into a man's drink and run away."

"The curer said that?"

"Yes. The one with the bird spirit in him."

Rego grimaced.

"The almighty curer again," he said.

"Why did you set the fire?" Kelkar asked.

"It wasn't me," Sal said.

"Where is the curer?"

Sal wagged his fingers above his head like wings.

"Flown," he said.

As soon as Kelkar chose the exit to Goi, he realized they were leaving Fins Island behind. And that he faced a jail term in a mainland prison.

"You promised to let me go," he cried out when he saw Kelkar grinning at him through the rear-view mirror.

Chapter 68

G *oi*

The police station was abuzz with action, and the seating area was full. Visitors sat on uneven benches, with many of them having been there for hours. For some, like the one hysterical woman with a balled-up scarf at her mouth, it was a painful wait. Her adult daughter had vanished without a trace, she said, crying out loud. The keening mother so annoyed a cop on duty, he ordered her to stop.

"If your missing girl hears your awful voice, she may never come back," he said.

The riposte produced a laugh from the public and his fellow cops. It broke the tension in the room. The day was routine for police officers at the station. They filed reports and followed up on leads. And answered questions from anxious relatives and demanded answers from them in return.

Kelkar was surprised to see his inbox empty. And he saw that the cork bulletin board on the wall was pinned with dated post its. Though he knew they had reassigned his pending cases, his too clean desktop threw him for a loop. This investigation was eating up his time.

He could use a cup of tea, he thought.

"The tea boy is here," his assistant Ferdy said with his head in the doorway as if reading his mind.

"Hot tea, Ferdy. Not lukewarm," he said.

A somber Ferdy nodded and disappeared outside. He hailed a passing tea boy on his afternoon rounds through the station and grabbed a cup of steaming tea from his tray. Ferdy gave him the tea and left. As he sipped, a sheen of cool sweat beaded across his forehead.

The phone at his desk rang at a pitch that urged him to drop whatever he was doing and pay attention. He let it jangle until he finished his tea, and then he answered the call. Souza was at the other end.

"There you are! I was ready to hang up the phone. Are you all wrapped up, Kelkar?" he said.

"Not quite," he replied.

"Close the damn case."

"I have information from a witness."

"Who is this witness?"

"A Kori."

"What has he told you?"

"Not much. He is not talking."

"Your decision. Spit into the wind or jump on that vacancy."

Kelkar scooped up a case file from his table and kept up a running stride until he reached the door.

"We have business on the island. Bring Sal's statement with you," Kelkar said to Rego.

"Got it," Rego said, trotting along to catch up with him.

"Sustenance first. Had any lunch yet?"

"Not yet," Rego said.

He started the car.

"Where to?" he asked Kelkar.

"Temperado. Where else?"

Chapter 69

ins Island
F   The doctor was at the center of the burned wreckage in the records room. A pasty film coated the entire floor and the crumpled shelving.

"Not all is lost," he said, pushing bits of seared wood around with his shoe tips. "Some of the evidence in steel cabinets has survived the fire. But, as you can see, it is a mess."

Kelkar singled out a photograph from the file. The doctor swept a magnifier over the bruise patch on Berto's face.

"Refresh my memory, detective. How did he get that bruise?" he asked.

"My witnesses said he landed on his cheek at the restaurant," he said.

"Was that the last time he was served a drink?"

"Correct. He went missing soon after."

"This is significant. When he fell, did the beer mug go down with him?"

"It did. The contents spilled during the fall."

"Your idea is verifiable."

"How?"

"With a reagent test. Our office followed protocol, and UV tested his clothes for urine and other bodily discharges. But not for atropine."

"The lethal alkaloid in *d. sattivus*."

"The toxin disappears in the human body, as I have said before. But if someone spiked his drink with atropine –,"

"And the liquid splashed onto his clothing –,"

"A fiber test may reveal traces."

"And strengthen the case."

"I wish I had thought of that," the doctor said with a smile.

Kelkar replayed Sal's statement for him.

"Sal is right," the doctor pointed out. "The curer can disappear with the greatest ease. He is a moving target and would be impossible to trap."

"We now know he meant to kill when he gave Sal the job."

"The question is - why did he poison Berto Souza?"

"Say our samples test positive for atropine."

"Changes everything."

"And fills in the blank - the manner of death - on your report."

"It becomes death by poison. Murder, in other words."

Chapter 70

G *oi* Souza's estate was at the fifty-mile marker on the map, in an area outside city limits. The load hauling trucks sped by on the opposite artery leading to the capital. There were no vehicles ahead or to the rear of them. The coiling ribbon of a road heaved between the checkered fields on both sides and leaped and bounded into the stark night.

Kelkar stared up at the sky. He never looked above the skyline while out in the city. Few urbanites did. And he saw how the absence of ambient lighting here had transformed the sky into the deepest, silkiest shade of black. Stars studded the milky way, weaving through the dark sky in spectacular contrast. There were no city lights here to mute the beauty of the constellations or overshadow them. In its element here, the starry firmament was matchless.

He took a detour from the major road and shifted onto a nubby, grit covered route. As the tires crunched forward, light jounced off white paint rings on tree trunks and served as beacons in the darkness.

Clear of the trees, giant sugarcane tracts with barrel-shaped stems shot upwards. He halted when a fugitive donkey marched through the overgrown forest of canes. The animal paused and glared cross-eyed into the light as if in a trance.

Rego got out. He waved his arms and shouted, but the massive donkey dug in its hooves instead. Head thrown back, it opened its jaws wide and brayed loud enough to wake up the dead.

They steered nearer, and the fugitive turned on a dime and disappeared into the fields. Saddle bells rang fast, slowed, and fell silent.

"The donkey menace," Rego said, collapsing with laughter.

"I thought donkeys were docile."

"You are thinking of sheep."

"Maybe I was."

"This one had a mind of its own."

"A cool fugitive donkey."

"What an animal."

Rego was confident the rutted road converted to a paved highway further. Kelkar had come to trust his sense of orientation, and he drove on. And just as he had said, they arrived at the concreted stretch of freeway half a mile after. He crossed the marker and merged onto an unincorporated road. A wire fence at the road's end stretched on either hand. The terrain past the fence was shaped by mounds of brush and spiny trees growing up a hill. High on the hill's ridge, a truck dipped and bounced as it went across, its fiendish headlights spearing the black with a razor sharpness.

Kelkar dimmed the lights.

"Veliz, the caretaker who keeps a vigil at night. It is prudent to move back now," Rego said quietly.

The caretaker's vehicle receded into the brushwood. Kelkar reversed and cut the engine.

"What do you have?" he asked Rego.

"Locals told me a pack of excavators maneuvered over that hill days ago," Rego said. "Souza comes by every night and leaves hours afterward. Stray cattle busted through a weak spot in the fence last week and Veliz got really upset by that. He warned neighbors he will kill any wayward flock on Souza property in the future."

"Is that unusual?"

"Strays posed no problems before. That's why his remark has caused tension among landowners here."

The truck traveled over the peak and down the other side. They jumped the fence. A smoggy glare from the summit outlined the ridge against the sky. They ran alongside the scrub and trees that offered cover and moved toward the top. Beyond the peak, the ridge slanted to about a thousand feet below. At the bottom, in a rectangular expanse, Souza and Lala relaxed on folding chairs. Behind the chairs, a pair of hurricane lamps on a post swayed and cast a web of flare and shadows on them. They clinked their drink glasses in a toast, and their heads bobbled closer as they carried on talking.

Crosswise from where they sat, excavators lay idle at a construction site between hillocks of turned-up dirt. Veliz approached from the site, and he stood by a makeshift tent near the men and smoked a cigarette in the dark. Their drinks done, Souza gave a shout out to him and Veliz lifted the canvas screen and entered the tent. Seconds later, floodlights blazed bright in the clearing. The light washed over the landscape until the smallest rock and pebble became as vivid as objects under a mighty sun.

From the heart of the brightness rose a vision. A magnificent marble city of standalone vaults emerged from a stone step-well. The main structure at the center was larger in comparison, with a soaring spire of gold on its cupola. Carvings of nymphs, charioteers, and warriors on the creamy Makrana marble had a motionless but stirring grace. Long passageways ran between the columned structures all around and unified at the vanishing point. It seemed to hover in the air, an illusion which could go 'poof' any minute. And they waited, thinking it must happen, it was too unreal. The floods flipped off and the image dissipated into the void in an instant as they expected. Lamps on the post flickered in the dark again. A dream vaporized, just as you wanted it to last a little longer.

They stopped at the fence and looked back when they heard the men hooting with laughter. The flashes from the floodlights waxed and waned from over the rim like perverse firebolts gone awry.

Chapter 71

The next day, he paid a visit to the research section at the city library to find out more. As he went through the literature on old landmarks and monuments, a certain Professor Anton DaCunha popped up often in academic citations. He stopped by the information desk to talk to the librarian restocking a shelf.

"The professor is the expert on historic places," she said.

"Never heard of him," Kelkar said.

"You don't watch the history channel, I suppose."

"Not much."

"The professor is all over it. Quite a local celebrity, he is. And charges by the minute, I heard," she said, and went back to the aisles.

Kelkar called the historian.

A short consultation, the suspicious DaCunha said, via his polite assistant. He declared himself a busy man with only an hour to spare, and Kelkar agreed to keep the meeting brief.

"Your one free hour begins now," the professor said disagreeably and with no preliminary chitchat. He lit a pipe and flopped into an armchair. A blue smoke cloud drifted by them, and a sickly-sweet smell flooded the room.

Their story galvanized the professor into action. He jumped up from his seat, a different man, and he rushed to where a contemporary map of Goi lay under heavy books. Fired up, and all smiles, he unfolded the map on the top of the pile. He compared it to older, historic records of the region. Then he circled and underlined sections with a pencil, going back and forth between diagrams. He crossed out or masked with tape some portions. When an inch of space remained on the map, he threw his pencil up in the air. He had pinpointed the sighting's exact location, he told them.

"Do you know of the Great Samudri quake, gentlemen?" the professor asked, drawing circles with his pipe stem to make the point.

"I read a vast city of vaults disappeared in 1750 after a tremor hit the region," Kelkar said.

"You are right. But let me start at the beginning. Five hundred years before the cataclysm occurred, the King of Samudri ruled the state. His dashing vizier, Mohun Garé, was a trusted inner circle member."

"And Peter Souza's direct ancestor."

"You did your homework."

"I did."

"Well, they say he had a recurring dream. Of a white marble city of vaults. The image so haunted him, he went to the king with a plan. It was decided in the court then to erect one just like the vision in his dream. The city was built underground with connecting passages that led to the sea. And it took twenty thousand workers fifteen years to complete."

"Then the earthquake happened."

"A calamitous upheaval that buried the descendant king's hopes and ambitions. With the city went the priceless coffers secured in the vaults by a line of royals and the wealthy. Everything got lost in the aftermath and passed into myth. The Samudri kingdom slipped from its former glory for a few years, but the king went on to win major battles. He refilled his war chests. And his reign was a successful one, culminating on a high note."

They watched him pull up the records on Antiquities Repository of Goyan History. He pivoted the screen.

"India is a land of many planned cities from the age of royals. One can resemble the other. Take your time. Examine the fine points. Is this what you saw?" he asked them, pointing to an artist's rendition of the site.

They moved nearer to have a look.

"What we saw that night was unlike any city. It was more of a marching line of intricate marble vaults," Kelkar said.

"Were there passageways like in this sketch?

"Yes, between each of the vaults."

"How closely does it match what you saw?"

"It's very close."

DaCunha became distant, removed from the present. He was traveling back to the past. And perhaps wishing he had witnessed the scene along with them that night.

Kelkar caught the look.

"I must remind you, professor. This is an ongoing investigation," he cautioned.

The professor raised a finger to his mouth. A wisp of a smile moved over his face, only to vanish in seconds.

"My lips are sealed," he said in an undertone.

The cloying odor still clung to their clothes when the session ended over two hours later. He rose from the chair, saying he would waive the extra charge, and he showed them the door.

Chapter 72

Angry farmers ramped up their criticism of Souza. They were deep in the red to begin with, but then his dithering, and his forgiveness of the fines Carnak owed Goi pushed them over the edge. Those concessions cost him dearly. The farm sector made it official and switched allegiance to Diem, the rising star on the political scene, and pinned their hopes on him. Diem was in a cushy position as a result of the switch by the bloc.

Close to election week, rainbands from the island's hurricane spiraled toward Goi. In days heavy showers gusted in and sopped parched fields, and the whole landscape disappeared under a waterfall of rain. Diem's followers saw the events as a sign that even nature was smiling on him.

A week of rain passed, and then in an event not witnessed for a long time, the Mithula River rose by feet instead of measly inches. His ecstatic supporters claimed it was another favorable omen from the heavens above. In the eyes of his allies, he had already won.

Companies that did business with farmers supported Diem, and the more he talked, the more they liked what he said. A staunch supporter was Agrow Bank which served farmers' commercial interests in Goi. The owner of the bank came from a farming community sorely tested by the drought, and he was no fan of the governor. He publicly stood with Diem. His vocal criticism had become a thorn in Souza's side.

One early morning, days before polling opened, disaster greeted tellers when they came to work at some of the branches. Vicious anti-Diem graffiti marked the walls. Smashed tables and chairs and trashed desks and office equipment had them shaken. A ragged trail of torn up Diem posters littered the room like bits of colored confetti.

The vandalism happened at other places that endorsed Diem, and in concert with the riots at his rallies. But his approval ratings rose in the polls despite the disruptions. Voters had wisened up.

As happens with life, the turmoil ended, and the next news cycle began. Elections took place with no glitches. Voters turned up in record numbers, and the sixty percent turnout shattered the state's previous polling records. When results arrived in the morning, Diem had scored forty out of fifty seats. It was an unprecedented landslide victory for the Alliance.

Chapter 73

Papery clouds stuck in a pattern fogged the capital for a few more days, but other than that the weather stayed dry. A milk truck started its rounds during those muggy dawn hours on its usual schedule, and as the driver drove into a fog bank, he hit what he thought was a fallen animal. He heard something go bumpity-bump. In the mist streaming by he saw a bundle roll into a ditch and he took his eyes off the road. In seconds he had lost control of the truck. The truck swerved, toppled a fire hydrant, and came to a full stop.

When he stepped out to check the bundle in the ditch, he discovered the bloodied corpse of Beluga Lala. He climbed back onto the truck with a mix of terror and pride coursing through him, convinced he had killed a notorious racketeer. After he had rested his forehead on the wheel for a while, he got a grip on himself and called the cops.

Water from the broken hydrant washed over Lala. The gush flowed onto the vacant streets and glistened with a macabre rinse of crimson. He was face down in the overflow, his limbs twisted in a cadaveric spasm, and with his fingers curled around a phone. And it looked as if he had tried calling for help while in the throes of death.

"Lala was stabbed with a *katar* late last night, or early this morning. It is chaos out here. Blood is everywhere," said Jo Tavares, the chief investigator at the station, who called to inform him.

"That is a dagger the Kori use," Kelkar said to him.

"It is the weapon of choice when they want a messy end."

215

"Did you find it?"

"Not yet."

"What's it like?"

"The *katar* is a thing of beauty forged by skilled sword smiths. They pass the craft down over generations. Takes them years to fashion the weapon. It has a killer, two-pronged undulating blade, about sixteen inches long. A quick stab of those sawtooth blades into soft tissue and you are a goner."

"Aren't they banned?"

"In many states. But not the islands. States banned them because the alloy used is so toxic, even superficial wounds never heal. Lala's body bears the characteristics of a classic *katar* dagger thrust. A mortal score in his case."

"Where can I find a one?"

"Not many in circulation at present. Owners guard their weapons zealously."

"How about in a weapons store or a museum?"

"I hate to say it, but they are all replicas. Not particularly good ones at that."

"Any clues on who killed him?"

"Casino employees and his family pointed at Souza. They said Lala had gotten in over his head once he became involved with him."

He told Tavares what they witnessed from the ridge top that night.

"None of his people we interviewed mentioned it," Tavares said. "Either they are lying, or Lala kept his mouth shut. I say there is ample cause for a warrant against Souza."

"What about Lala's phone?"

"Have it. It is part of the evidence. If they talked before he got bumped, we will soon know."

As he ended his discussion with Tavares, he picked up loud cries coming from the direction of the jail cells. He heard the rush of guards running along the hallway. Before he made it to the door, one of them burst through the room and ran up to his desk.

"Sal Bilbao's dead. He hanged himself," he whispered.

Kelkar and the guards hurried to the cell block. Sal hung by his prison clothes to the bars of a window facing a cinderblock wall. He touched the remains. His extremities had sustained warmth and color, the tissue in general had retained its normal shape and the neck region was clear and unmarked by the fabric. When forensics finished, he had a word with the investigator.

"Nearly all cases of self-inflicted asphyxiations have markings on the upper neck. Not in this case," the investigator said.

"A tad too flawless, no?" Kelkar said.

"An anomaly. But."

He swept away the hair from the back of the neck and pointed at puncture marks on the base of occiput.

"Make a wild guess."

"A four-pointed Girter bite," Kelkar said, dumbstruck.

A Girter was the deadliest krait in these parts. The venom worked in less than two seconds. Delivered death to the victim in five seconds max. There was no mistaking a Girter bite.

"The snake was smuggled in and latched to the skull by a human hand."

"That part of the body would be impossible for a snake to access."

"Bingo."

"Don't they leave fangs in the victim after a strike?"

"Four solenoglyphous fangs were embedded in the scalp. We got them."

"A planned hit."

"You got that right."

"Could be a lifer who did it. What does he have to lose?"

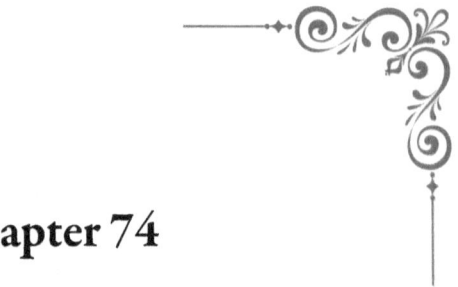

Chapter 74

"Detective Kelkar," the new police commissioner Melvin Paes said.

Paes had summoned him to his office for an update on the investigation. Diem had wasted no time appointing his own trusted people, and Paes was his early pick. He was brusque and direct, a war veteran, and neither invited nor shied away from controversy.

"At your service," Kelkar replied.

"A friend of Souza."

"We go back."

"Still holding hands with him?" he asked.

"Doing my job, Commissioner," he said.

"Good answer."

Kelkar laid out the evidence they had gathered in front of him.

"Do you remember the Treasures Act of 1797?" Kelkar said.

"It was replaced by Souza, was it not?" Paes replied.

"Souza pushed to overturn the Act. And he did," he pointed out to Paes.

"The Treasures Act was archaic, and out of touch with modern times. Everybody agreed on that."

Under the Act, any historical edifice, structure, or coin dated over a hundred years - and discovered on private land - went to the state. Deed owners got nothing. And the state imposed severe penalties on those who flouted the law.

"He replaced it with the Finders Keepers Bill. During the elections."

Souza introduced the new bill close to his term's end. It was when the elections had dominated airways, and at a tumultuous time in the state.

He insisted all findings belonged solely to the deed owners, the citizens. Why should the state grab it all? He thundered that point at the lectern and argued for the bill, but he need not have bothered. Stressed members chasing election news had not read the thousand-page bill. They were too busy on their cell phones planted out of view of cameras, and they ignored the speech. He received only a smattering of applause.

"It was an absurd bill nobody cared about!" Paes said.

The legislators had bickered at the session that the proceedings were a waste of taxpayer money. They said no Goyan was going to get filthy rich off a find. And that old treasures in Goi were scant, with none in recent history. Rare finds were just that - rare. So they gave the bill their unanimous consent, passed it into law, and went home.

"Perhaps they should have," Kelkar said. "I mean, in light of the discovery."

His linking of the two events horrified Paes. He fully grasped the extent to which Souza had blindsided them.

"The damned trickster!" he exclaimed.

"He recruited Lala for his dirty work in the initial phase," Kelkar said. "They turned into bosom buddies after and talked daily."

Paes gave a skeptical grunt.

"And when the legislation passed, he decided Lala knew too much. He had outlived his usefulness," he said.

"Maybe. We are still putting all the pieces of the puzzle together," Kelkar said.

Paes slapped his palm on the desk. His thick brows beetled.

"Do whatever it takes. Get the bastard," he said. "Souza's party has relied on the force of his will and little else for too long."

Kelkar held his tongue. Evidence in a case was the real naked emperor. The chips must fall as they may, the same as with all his cases.

Chapter 75

The walkway skirted the lake and rolled up the hill to the house. It was hushed up here. Kelkar could hear the random rain from a trolling cloud stipple the lake. The water flared in circles all the way to the farthest bank from him. At the edges, a solitary crane stood on stilted legs between floating lily pads, stalking its prey. There was a sudden whoosh of beating wings, and he stopped to watch flamingoes aflame in a ray of light touch ground with a dainty precariousness. The scene below him had the quality of a pastoral painting, at odds with the turbulence surrounding Souza.

When his knocks received no response, he circled the house and pried a bathroom window free. He vaulted in. A long hallway stretched past the room, and from the wide doors at the end, dialogue from a movie played on the television. He crept forward toward the sounds. In the room, Souza sat with a drink in hand on a couch in front of the screen. As Kelkar stepped through, he looked up in confusion.

"What brings you here?" Souza said to him.

"Lala is dead. He was knifed and dumped outside his casino. I am to take you in for questioning," he said.

"He was a thief," Souza said, slurring the words.

"We located the buried city on your land. Though you hid it well, we are on the case."

"That is but a shell. Inside lies history," Souza said, with a cunning laugh. "You will never guess what we discovered in the depositories. Artifacts so splendid I dreamed about them for days. Asleep and awake!

Best thing I did? I scrapped the useless Treasures Act before I lost. And with my bill's passing, it is mine."

"Did Berto know?" he asked.

"I had no intention of telling him," Souza said with a dismissive motion. "People manipulated Berto. Like taking candy from a baby. He would have squandered it all."

"What happened between you and Lala?"

"We had a deal. He was to excavate the property under my supervision. And rabble rouse, make trouble for Diem, and sway the vote any way he could."

"And you repaid him what Berto owed, so he gave up the chase."

"We settled his debt, yes. I paid him an advance and the rest was to be decided later. But the treasure got to his crook brain. Veliz said he caught him pocketing gold coins one night. He had the nerve to steal. From me! It drove me into such a fury, I handed Veliz the orders. He did what I told him to do."

"Where is the find?"

"Veliz guards it for me."

"I would not trust him if I were you."

"Ah, but I must! He is family. My great-grandfather, Leon Souza, had children from a Kori girl, and he comes from that strain. From my island side. Veliz is solid."

Souza waved his arm at the television screen with a bittersweet look. He had seen this movie so often he mouthed the actors' lines and whooped in jubilation when he got it right.

"Our favorite movie when Berto and I were kids," he said. "But siblings change when they grow up, don't they? He turned out to be a sniveling loser. Always extending his hands for my money."

"Did you have him murdered?"

Souza's eyes glassed over with incomprehension.

"He died from heart failure. And all that heavy drinking destroyed his insides. The good-for-nothing! Didn't you read his autopsy report?" he said.

"He died after he ingested a poison slipped in his drink," Kelkar replied. "The ME has determined his death a murder. That is the latest."

Souza teetered on the lip of an abyss and in front of a terrible truth.

"What do you mean?" he said. The news sunk in, and he seemed to wither with disbelief. "It was not Lala! It was -"

He wheezed from the impact of a stem thin arrow that shot through the window. His breath abandoned him before he completed the sentence. The projectile flew with such swiftness, it struck him in his chest and killed him in an instant. Kelkar saw it too late.

He rushed to the open window and stared into the rain, wiping the drops trickling down his face. The timid rain became a viscous deluge and flattened the trees. Leafy branches curved earthward from the onslaught of water and drenched parrots struggled up in alarm from the canopy, disturbed by happenings only they could see.

With Souza dead, authorities swarmed the city site and located an underground system of vaults and crypts just as he had boasted. The foot thick granite doors of about a hundred odd chambers had all been blown up and destroyed. The vaults were empty.

Chapter 76

Fins Island
Naini slid out of bed, and she slipped on a tunic and loose pants. She wrapped a scarf on her head to conceal her long hair. When she was at the door she hesitated for an instant, and then she stole out without a backward glance. Moments later, she was at the front entrance. Smudges of lilac tinged the sky in the east, the rest of the earth lay under a weighted blanket of darkness. From the corner of the house, she watched the security guards march into the dark and disappear around the bend. She threw her sandals over the gates, clambered up the horizontal rails, and landed on the other side.

It was a short walk to the town's bus terminal, where she bought a ticket to Mumbai at the ticketing booth. The dozy clerk at the window addressed her as 'sir' when he handed her the receipt and she guessed it was because of her clothing. She giggled at his presumption, at her cleverness with the disguise. Her reaction did not amuse him, however. He did not get the joke, and ignoring her, he looked past her to the next in line.

"Next!" he said, sliding the change into the tray with a clank, and more awake now.

Sellers who had arrived before sunrise readied their food stalls at the terminal. They unlocked cabinets, fired stoves, and set griddles that sizzled with oil on burners. Fried sweets, savory delicacies, and crispy snacks filled counters. Kettles of hot tea on compact stands steamed in the cool morning. As vendors wheeled carts loaded with hourglass shaped bottles of soda, the liquid sloshed the glass. Up and down the bottles they went like prancing rainbow beams.

And then, before you knew it, people appeared. Straggly ant lines of travelers waited at shops, ticket windows and water fountains. By the curb, sure-footed passengers shimmied up ladders and onto roofs of buses and parked themselves there along with their belongings. The lumbering vehicles squawked to life, and black smoke blew out their exhausts as they pulled out of the depot. Smells of diesel and tempered mustard oil swirled through the air.

A shaved ice vendor pushing his cart sounded an air horn, and she rushed to buy the treat. The jars of raspberry, orange, strawberry, mango, tamarind, mint, and sweet lime syrups in the cart were enticing. She shifted from foot to foot, and after a minute's pondering she chose the tamarind ice.

The vendor fashioned the shavings into a mound and placed the concoction in a cup. He then poured the gooey syrup in ribbons, saturating the slush till it became a deep shade of purple liquorice. As she slurped at the ice, her jaws seized with cold, and her teeth grew numb. Yet she could not eat the slurry of ice fast enough. The treacly sour syrup had an aftertaste that danced in her mouth.

Things were looking up for her, and she could hardly wait for the journey to begin. She was on her way to shining Mumbai on the bus, a city whose lights never dulled. That was the fairytale of spun sugar told and retold in a million movies she had seen and reseen, and she had believed in that story all her life. The image of a city of light burned so bright in her imagination it had assumed a life of its own. And her expectations fizzed, bubbled, and brimmed over.

Her aunt from Vanati had moved to Mumbai after she quit her resort job. She now worked at a garment company in Dharavi, a large enterprising slum in the financial capital. One of thousands of businesses, the firm had grown from a small workshop to an international export house. The firm needed workers her aunt had said when they last talked, and she persuaded her to visit and try for a job there.

Naini undid her scarf, and she combed her long hair and tied it loosely at her nape. Then she put on her glass bangles, feeling like herself once again. She hummed a riff from *Heart's Song*, a movie where Sundari plays a guileless heroine who pines for a fanciful love.

"Am I with you or is it fancy?
I hear but cannot see
The enchanted bird singing.
Playful night
Tiptoes in.
Stay with me for a while."

The hawkish man at a tea stall shadowed her until she boarded the bus. Then he sauntered away and made a call.

"Naini's on the move. She is on the road to Mumbai," he said.

"Let her go, she is off the hook," Kelkar said to him.

Chapter 77

Ladies dressed in festive colors waited at the entrance, nattering among themselves. Bright circles of calendula flower garlands were looped over their forearms. The sunburst orange flowers were symbolic of farewells, and a goodwill token for the departing guests on their way to their destinations.

Bir avoided the twittering front office ladies, hurrying past them and on to the parked taxicab. He was eager to make an inconspicuous getaway and begin his vacation at a paternal uncle's home in Kolkata. The sharp-eyed women noticed when he stole by them and puckish smiles lit their faces. He was mortified by their amusement, certain it was about him, and he pressed the cabbie to get going. But the vehicle refused to start, which further annoyed Bir.

The driver assured him all was well. He dug out a spanner from the trunk and popped the hood. Then he tinkered with mechanisms, making decisive clanging noises. All the while, he kept up a running commentary on how he could fix anything. He wiped the smut off his hands with a rag, touched the gold amulet slung on his visor, and muttered a prayer. The engine stammered, hiccupped a little, and came back to life. Bir was finally off to his destination to his relief.

Meanwhile, Jha distributed brochures to guests before they left for the airport.

"Looking good, Mr. Rumbler," he said to Herb, who was a few pounds lighter at the end of the retreat.

"We are returning next year, you know," Herb said, flapping the brochure at him. He had his other arm around Claudia, who gazed up at him sweetly.

"I am most pleasurable to perceive you again," Jha said. He moved on to the other guests.

"You can take carrom board with yourselves for playing at your house since you have enjoyed too much I observed. There is two ones there," he said to Greg and Vikki heaving their suitcases over the steps.

"Noooo! My bag is full," Vikki groaned.

"Teasing. Next visit come with extra empty suitcase," he said to them.

They chuckled and said they might.

"And you, sir?" he asked Pravesh who looked away from him and did not respond.

"Some people these days. Can nod and say yes, no or who knows."

Sandy was searching for the always evanescent cuckoo bird in a tree nearby.

"Are you not agreeing with myself, Miss Tauno?" he mumbled to her.

"I am sorry, Mr. Jha. You were saying?" she said, sounding vague.

"It was not small bit extraordinary. I am asking if we meet you on one more retreat," he said to her.

"I would love to return," she said, and she took the brochure he handed her.

"That is what I am calling a very well reply," he said, beaming at her. Then he shooed all of them toward the shuttle and waved them on, his manner hearty as usual.

"Go, the whole of you guests. You must not be missing proper flights."

He darted a sly look at Rish who stood beside him on the front porch.

"You are not seeming your normal self this sunniest morning, Mr. Tilak. Is all fine and dandy with you?" he said.

An irritable line indented Rish's brow. He disregarded the remark and focused instead on the landscape. Yet again, he wondered why he tolerated the man.

"What happened to all the calendula flowers, Jha?"

The flower beds were crowded with blossoms in every hue but orange.

A stumped Jha called Jass over with a shout.

"The esteemed Mr. Tilak here is inquiring important things of you. What happened to all cal and ulla flowers and orangey coloring on the premises?" he asked the head gardener.

"I made garlands like you told me to," Jass said, appearing confused.

Jha glowered at him. He pointed at the rose bushes to distract the gardener's attention.

"What flowers are those?" he asked him.

Jass produced a pair of clippers from his pocket. He clipped the dusky pink roses off the stems and sliced the thorns before he presented the bunch to Rish.

"These are island damask roses," he said.

"So much so better than common cals and ullas," Jha sniffed.

He glared a warning at Jass in case he blurted out something careless.

The roses were close to bloom, with delicate petals that folded in on each other. Rish breathed in their luxurious fragrance, the flowers so velvety soft on his skin. He turned away with a gruff sigh.

Chapter 78

About the length of a pencil, the projectile tapered to the size of a pinhead. The nock at the bottom bore the same vined inscription as the one scored on Berto Souza.

"Watch out," Kelkar cautioned the doctor.

"The poison has to puncture skin or be ingested to cause harm," Dr. Sahu said. But even as he said that he placed the dart back in the box with care.

"That infernal etching," Kelkar said.

"Any ideas on who killed Souza?"

"The inscription bears the Kori stamp."

"This is a curer's dart."

"He melted away, despite us having a team on standby. The shot came from higher ground, from over the treetops. It flew straight through the window."

The doctor pointed at the rain trees outside that mushroomed in a thick canopy to the horizon.

"Years ago, a street performer and his trained monkey landed by ferry on Fins Island," he said. "We have no monkey species on the island, in case you wondered."

"I did wonder," Kelkar said with a laugh.

"The animal broke free from its master and disappeared into the surrounding forest. Days after, people spotted him a hundred miles across. He made it by jumping through the contiguous tree canopy here."

"You think the curer does that?" Kelkar asked.

"It is an idea to consider," he replied.

"The Kori say he lives in the trees but is invisible. And that he can fly over land and water. Is he for real, though?"

"You might find out."

"I meet with their leader this afternoon."

"Hope he talks."

"Does this dart carry the same toxin?"

"It most certainly does. You might have saved yourself a trip. The toxicology lab in Goi can run tests too."

"The lab suggested I bring it here. To the expert."

"I suspect the dart is coated with a tropane alkaloid."

"The same substance as in *d. sattivus.*"

"Right. Curers have utilized the very same one for centuries. Historical evidence shows they use the berries to kill."

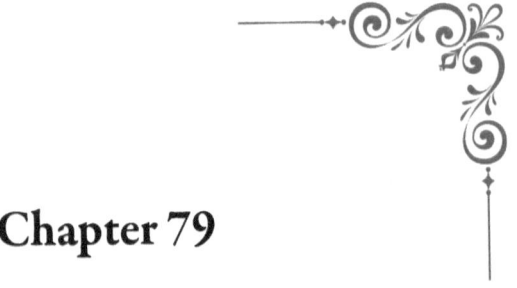

Chapter 79

They were in Pavim to meet with the Kori leader, Tamrin Sibil.

"Where is Veliz?" Kelkar asked him when they walked into his office.

Sibil's square face was expressionless. He was a corpulent man, and his flab bulged in involuted rolls from the borders of the cushioned chair. The armrests creaked and squeaked with his bulk.

"There is nobody called Veliz here," he said outright. "You police are criminals. Liable for murder. One of my people was finished in your jail cell."

His anger animated him, lifting him off his seat with an agility he otherwise lacked.

"You mean Sal Bilbao?"

"Yes, yes, Sal Bilbao. You police dragged him to Goi. For what crime?"

"For murder, Mr. Sibil. Administering deadly poison to a human is a crime in all states and territories. As for his death, it is under investigation. The perpetrators will be punished, I assure you."

"He did no such thing. Where is the proof?"

"We have his sworn recorded statement as proof. I suggest you wait until the trial before you judge."

"There is no Veliz here," he insisted.

"And the curer?"

Sibil pointed upwards and yawned. His arms flagged over the rests; his eyelids drifted down. He sank onto the chair with his chin to his chest and he began to snore. They looked over Sibil's dipped head. As he slept, a screensaver had flicked on at the computer on his desk. A photograph of grave tribals, sitting in a stilted placement for the picture taker, rolled on the screen. They moved forward for a better glimpse.

Veliz was attired in full tribal regalia in the picture. And he stood with none other than Sibil himself. The burly Sibil seated on a teak throne cut an imposing figure. But it was the weapon Veliz displayed that astounded them. He held the distinctive *katar* or scorpion dagger, like the one police said killed Lala. That Sibil knew him was certain, though Kelkar doubted he would cooperate. This trip had cost them time. It was imperative they find Veliz before they lost him again.

As they reached the door, a man with red lac painted on his veined limbs blocked their exit. His face spread into a ferrety smile.

"Tell Sibil we will return. Maybe next time he will stay alert and deal," Kelkar said to the hostile man.

Meanwhile, Sibil stirred awake on hearing their voices. He spoke a few peremptory words in a dialect to the man who stepped aside and let them pass. Outside the office, angry men, women, and children converged in a greater mob. The crowd pressed onward, driving them back until they retraced their steps and left Pavim behind.

Rego checked his phone and led the way.

"Our tracker has spotted Veliz, sir. He is headed to Kori Cave," he said.

"And you mapped the route?" Kelkar said.

"I put the map up here," Rego said, tapping his forehead. "Reception is spotty under the trees."

"Heh," Kelkar said.

Rego waved his phone at him.

"Dead as a doorknob," he said with a grin.

They widened their strides until they arrived at the nailed sign pointing the other way from Pavim. A sharp turn later, the terrain changed to a capricious stairway of moss-covered rocks, and past the

233

rocky slope a bridge of knotted lianas was strung across a ravine. They crossed the bridge of vines. The trail then climbed higher and steeper, winding downwards again through gigantic raintrees. Water droplets seeped from the raintree pods, and they breathed a mix of loamy mist and bog air.

Kori Cave lay east of Pavim. The cave blended with the perpetual shadows of the prehistoric forest and was hard to locate, and one could walk right past and miss it. After some off-track turns, Rego found the gateway. They stopped a quarter of a mile from the gate, at the banks of the river Nara. The river poured into the mouth of the cave, and they could see the only way in was with a boat.

A blue azurite salt oozed from the cavern sides and mixed with the river as it waved through the cavern. And then, somewhere at the center, the dazing indigo Nara disappeared inside the earth. It was thought the waters flowed underneath the rock and emptied in the Indian Ocean at the island's southernmost tip. The place was sacred to the Kori.

In more truculent times, Goyan kings banished criminals and traitors to this, the dankest of prisons. Barred dungeons on the inner walls had just enough space for one inmate, and prisoners often spent the rest of their lives in the choking cells. The corroded iron fastenings that had bound them were yet there, melded over time to the calcified stone. Evil, wretched and innocent ghosts of the dead all trapped together in the stone for eternity.

From a granite outcropping on the river's bank, they saw the indistinct shapes of rowboats moored to tying posts. A mild wind blew crosswise and moved the water, and the hulls bumped together in a cadence. They crouched at the volcanic backdrop with a view of the entrance to pass the hours.

At midnight came the unmistakable sound of someone wading through the river. The splashes grew louder, and then the phantom outline of a man appeared at the wharf. He untied a boat and lit a paraffin torch, placing it in a receptacle at front. Oars slapped the river's plane as he rowed by them, and they recognized Veliz in the torch's light. They tailed him in a second boat, rowing beyond the lighted torches attached to the stony flanks.

The salt walls of the cave were tinted in the blues and violets of a cloudless twilight sky. A diverging tunnel led to a cavernous hall with a stone promontory at the left. Way above their heads, forsaken bird nests wainscoted the domed roof in the honeycomb patterns of a beehive. A crack of sound ran from end to end across the dome, like a scampering animal running for cover. They glanced up to see blue dust fall in a wave to the water below. The gnarled knotholes of the hive on the roof seemed to be watching and moving with them.

Veliz dropped anchor at the dock, and he leaped onto the landing stage. He wound a rope submerged at the other end at a rock bollard. They maneuvered their boat closer.

"Fishing for gold?" Kelkar shouted, cupping his hands around his mouth.

Veliz stumbled backwards when he saw them and keeled over. He scrambled on all fours and flung the rope loops over the dock's edge. The ponderous load of underwater cargo hit the bottom with a muffled thud. A swell raised their boat's bow and lowered the craft with a thwack, but they hung steady and then jumped onto the dock.

Chapter 80

Divers hauled more than five hundred oilcloth bags from the waters of Kori Cave. The eye-popping find floored the team. In there were custom-made toys of solid gold created for an offering during holy rites. For a godly favor, and not as a plaything for a child. There were gem-encrusted ceremonial daggers with blunted edges. And outmoded antique jewelry too heavy for anyone to wear. Rough diamonds as large as pigeon eggs and uncut sapphires crammed jewelry boxes. There were exquisitely cut emeralds and rubies with enigmatic depths to them. They recognized wealthy donors from engraved names on items, while others were complete riddles.

The kingdom's war chests of gold and silver coinage were the most difficult to salvage on account of the weight, but in the end they got those too. Under the recent law, Souza's widow Indu inherited it all.

The reclaimed fortune caused an uproar in the state assembly. Members realized the repercussions of the Finders Keepers Act and they were big mad.

Diem saw an opportunity in the situation. He sprang to the occasion, excited to wield his newly acquired powers and play the hero. And the same dull legislators who passed the now controversial bill drafted by Souza dove into the fray along with Diem. They told her that the Finders Keepers Act was crafted by deceit and maintained that the monumental find belonged in a national museum. That was its rightful place.

But she understood the poseurs for what they were. She would meet them in court, she said. And she vowed to ship her property to the Azores where she owned sizable land holdings. The tug-of-war between the administration and her lawyers dragged on in the public eye and showed no signs of stopping. Until fate cast a wrench in the works.

Three months later, news came out of the blue that she had passed away. Reports said the widow who was intractable to the end had died in her sleep of natural causes. The Souzas had left no offspring behind or suitable heirs, and as a matter of law, the state claimed their entire estate, including the find.

History Reclamation Department officials swooped down to the dozens of Souza properties, ready to take possession of what now belonged to the state. The herd did not find the historic cache anywhere. Walls were torn, the lake was dredged, and every bit of paper with a number on it seized as evidence. Still, no clues were found. The trove had disappeared like sand grains through a crevice in the earth.

Newspapers needed the story to go on because it was easy money. Their rumor mills began the grind, and the tabloids baked hot bread with the flour and sold it to their readers. Some speculated that the widow detested the Diem regime, and that she had returned the donations back to the descendants of donors rather than hand it over to the state. Others said she sold them piecemeal to private museums.

One report said she dropped the treasure in the Azorean seas, while another said she chucked it in the Indian Ocean. It was never quite clear what was true and what was not. Now and then stories floated in the ether of social media like bubbles and popped. They ebbed and flowed with the tide. But through it all, the faithful believed in the vanishing and insisted the truth was out there somewhere. Perhaps in some faraway sea or miles belowground in a foreign land, waiting to be discovered.

Chapter 81

G *oi* "You have one week," the presiding judge said to Kelkar before he adjourned the session.

The order came with strict instructions to move matters along and get Veliz to talk. Time passed. A day slipped into the next, and Kelkar feared the tribe would finish him before he uttered a single word. It was on the last day of that week, at the final interrogation, that things went all the way.

"Well, we meet again to dance to the same tune. The prosecutor tells me you are in for four murders," Kelkar said.

"I told you. I was not involved," Veliz insisted.

The former caretaker was his usual stolid self, but a slight shake of his wrist cuffs betrayed him.

"You plotted with the tribe. Poisoned Berto with the curer's help."

"It was not me. The boss used the tribe for his own benefit."

"That is a lie. He believed Berto met a natural end."

"He did not want to share his hoard. It was not me."

"It was you. Souza was greedy, but no killer. And he realized too late what a snake you are."

"It was not me!"

"You eliminated Lala with a *katar*."

"Not true."

"Two lifers you hired killed Sal with a Girter bite and hung him to the bars. If he had cooperated with police your goose would have been cooked."

"Sal was a tribal. I never would do that to him."

"You would do that. And you did. The curer fired an arrow dipped in the same poison into Souza's heart. That was the finale. With the brothers dead, you had their wealth. Four murders if you are counting."

"I didn't do it."

He held up the Salten feather.

"This belongs to an extinct bird."

Veliz twisted his arms through the shackles.

"It belongs to the Kori," he cried.

"Nobody but a curer can wear these in a warmask," Kelkar said.

He then replayed portions of Sec's testimony given after police booked him.

"And that is from an eyewitness who saw the curer near Berto's body."

Kelkar stopped the playback.

"Nowhere to run, nowhere to hide," he said.

Veliz struggled to his feet.

"Sit down, I am not done," Kelkar said. "Let me remind you again. You are neck-deep in shit, your hands wedged in your armpits with glue. It is the tribe or you. Save yourself before it is too late."

"You can't put me in a prison."

"You want this to end? Talk. I have all day."

"I did nothing."

"Here's the deal. Give us the curer's location. Then your life in jail may become more bearable. Maybe an occasional shave. Or an extra meal. Your kin have marked you with a bull's eye and you are in danger in prison and outside. So maybe some protection."

Veliz didn't say much for a long time. When he talked again, his voice was a strained whisper.

"On the night of the summer solstice festival," he said.

"What about it?" Kelkar asked.

"He touches ground at the eleventh hour at night," he said. "Wait until he has drunk at least three cups of the old earth healer's brew. You might have a slim chance then."

Chapter 82

Fins Island
The sign tacked to the tree was gone. Kelkar rubbed at the scored bark, removed the remaining bent nail and tossed it into the brush. He knew Pavim was west of where they stood. The agents grouped together at the start of the narrow path with their heads bent over the maps on the hood.

He led the way into the dark tree cover. It took the squad an hour of steady walking before the undergrowth thinned and the path broadened. They arrived at a large semicircle of free space, the same mud-tamped clearing where they captured Sal Bilbao.

The darkness was complete here. They skulked nearer to the settlement, to the square shapes of adobe homes that showed lighter than the shadows of the forest. The whooping cry of a nearby night heron had them on alert, but they heard no human sounds or voices. No fires belched smoke up the chimneys, no smells of food lingered in the air. The henhouses in the wood-fenced courtyards stood bare. Open doors and windows of homes chafed against the walls as a wind blew past. There was nobody there.

"Turn back. They have left," he said, signaling the crew.

Out in the public grasslands, a soft light still held. The flaxen sun sank over the clouds toward the hazy-hot edge of the sky. A young boy with a sturdy stick emerged from the windblown grass, herding his group of snuffling cattle toward them. Their grazing over for the day, the charging flock was going home to the stockyard for the night. Dust from hooves lifted in a cloud, and the dusty light filtered through their hairy humps and ears.

Kelkar stopped the boy.

"Where did the Kori go?" he asked him.

"They went there," he said, pointing north.

"Across the sea?"

"In their boats, to the forgotten islands."

He wheeled around, swearing, his expression grim. The forgotten islands were strewn like a pearl strand along the Indus Trough, about four hundred nautical miles from the mainland. Beyond their authority, and in dangerous waters. The Duros, a hostile tribe related to the Kori lived there. And a sure death awaited trespassers who ventured anywhere near.

The trail had dead ended. At least for now.

On his drive back to the mainland he pulled off the highway and over to a tea stall at the wayside. He ordered the super special. The vendor set the pot to boil with water, milk, and a generous spoon of black-leafed tea. He dropped a sachet of spice into the pot. The boiled tea was bitter but pleasant, with a bite of mace and star anise, and he savored the exhilarating taste of the drink and the smooth jolt from the caffeine.

His gaze fixed at the horizon's rim, at the gradual drift of lighted oil tankers making their passage over the sea. Ahead of him the Indian Ocean stretched far and wide and into the inky night. Cottony cumulous clouds floated by a wan moon and filled the sky. Then came a bleak call from above. He watched a bird shadow with clean wing lines fly behind a silver cloud. Northwards, and as swift as an arrow released from a taut bowstring. The mirage reappeared in the gaps and vanished. He stared until his eyes burned.

Chapter 83

G*oi*

He arrived at the station the next day and there was a flat folder propped in his inbox. A scrawled note from the police chief was stuck to the cover. His assignment in Larabos Island started tomorrow, the note said, and that they had booked his seat for the night. Before he flew out, he handed the investigation over to Rego so he could tie loose ends and complete any paperwork left.

At midnight, he boarded a cargo plane to the island along with another agent. The plane landed on schedule on a stunted runway, constructed between a row of craggy hills on the island's windward side. A short walk to the airport gates was like stepping inside a rolling mist, and the clammy air smelled of sulfur before a rainstorm. That damp odor of low clouds reminded him of Goi at the onset of monsoon season. A fat drop fell on him, and then a few more. He put on his jacket, secured his hood, and tightened the wrist snaps. How he hated the rain.

The Laraban undercover officers picked them up in the lobby. And they drove ten hours straight by way of a swampy forest dogging a shipment of narcotics. The chase went on through a hurried supper in the dark on the truck and less than forty winks of shut eye, and was repeated day after day, and night after night. When he returned to Goi one grueling year later, he was eager for details from Rego.

"What of Sec and Thak?" he asked Rego when they met at Borani's.

"Sec was indicted for tampering with evidence," Rego said. "He is in Bolim jail, which is still under Fereira."

"And Thak?"

"Believe it or not, Thak is a royal from Larabos Island."

"Could have fooled me."

"His panicked relatives pulled strings in the capital for his release. And the government agreed. They deported him but impounded his passport."

"Nice."

"Any word on their dear uncle?"

"Chacha fled to Nepal, evading prison by a whisker. But authorities seized that beachfront mansion he bought with drug money. He is gone for good."

"Better."

Rustomji brought cardamom tea and lamb fritters with mint chutney to their table. While Rego ate, he opened the day's Goyan Times. The island edition reported the Finsian governor had appointed a special commission to root out corruption in the government. Dr. Deb Sahu was the foremost expert on the panel, the report said. That was good news, and he texted his best wishes to the doctor.

He ordered a refill of tea and scanned the headlines.

A write-up on Mira Tilak caught his attention. The story speculated on her move to the capital which had caused a buzz in political circles. News broke that she may contest elections in the coming year from Peter Souza's constituency. Some said she might even front a candidate for the party.

He blew vapor off the cup and sipped the creamy black tea. The hooking power of politics, he mused. It was difficult for some to step off the merry-go-round.

He then turned to the daily's last page, the section with marginal news of the city. Boring stuff got published here, like store ribbon-cuttings, road detours and mosquito control in wards and such, but he read the page anyway. He stopped at a piece of news there.

It said a certain MV Foundation purchased 15,000 open acres near the historic buried city over an interval of months. The foundation had begun construction on wider roads, modern bridges, drought reservoirs and schools for the area. And would offer support to all Front political candidates at the district level according to their spokesperson, Ronnie Barbosa.

A river of money was making its way to the sea of politics.

He remembered the name, having chatted with the man during the investigation's course. Barbosa had told him he was moving to Goi, and to a new job at a firm that also owned Margosa. He said a deep-pocketed somebody planned big ventures for the state, though he gave no names.

"Remember the secretive foundation Sid Tito was running?" Rego said.

"It is the back page news of the day. On purpose."

"I dug deeper."

"They bought Souza's land?"

"They did."

Amused by the subtext of the two stories, he read between the lines. He considered the article again, at what remained unsaid. Front loyalists lived in and around that region, and they had voted for Souza in each election except the most recent one. Her timing was impeccable.

"The coming election should be interesting," he said.

He got himself another refill of tea.

He forgot the madness of the city in Borem Bay, a serpentine curve of beach on the island's west coast. His nearest neighbors lived miles away, with the sea and shore stretching as far as he could see.

The bay's desolation sprung him a fey surprise sometimes. Like the day a feral cat appeared from behind the scrub with a small minnow held fast in its jaws. The cat stepped forward on velvet paws and watched, ready to run for cover at a single wrong move from him. It looked as untamed as the bay, a natural in the place.

When he whistled low, the cat dropped its catch and meowed, and the sound was equal parts purr and growl. It grew into a daily ritual, with feline and prey stopping by for a visit in the mornings. And by and by the tawny cat adopted him.

The waves rolled onto the sands and their measured patterns brought up other happy memories by the sea. Blissed out, he drifted into sleep. Seconds later, his cell phone beeped. He picked it up and squinted at the screen. It was the commissioner calling.

"I realize you are on vacation, Kelkar. But this cannot wait," Paes bellowed from the other end. "My dear friend Bunny Pinto's mother has gone missing from her retirement home. Between you and me, the old battle-axe is better lost than found. But I owe Bunny a favor. We must locate her at once.

THE UPTURNING

Cast of Characters
On Fins Island
Rish Tilak – Margosa's director
Tara Shaw –health clinic manager
Selvam Kair - spa manager
Bir Munshi - yoga teacher
Mira Tilak – Rish Tilak's mother
P. Jha - office manager
Ronnie Barbosa - public relations manager
Naini - a runaway
Jass - head gardener
Tinnu Chacha – a drug lord
Sec - drug dealer who works for Chacha
Thak - drug dealer who works for Chacha
Sabine Parker - companion to Sec
Savio Fereira – police officer
Al Delgado - Sizzle restaurant owner
Jude Mascarenha - scuba diving business owner
Johnny - Jude's assistant
Sal Bilbao - Kori tribal
Tamrin Sibil - Kori tribal chief
The Curer
Yoga retreat visitors
Greg Bilisk
Vikki
Herb and Claudia Rumbler
Pravesh Doss
Sandy Tauno
In Goi
Peter Souza - Governor of Goi
Berto Souza - Peter Souza's brother

Carmel Diem - opposition leader
Veliz – Souza's caretaker
Vishal Batti - lawyer
Beluga Lala - mobster
Jiva Kelkar - Detective
Xavier Rego - Kelkar's deputy
Exit - police informant
Deni Shood - liquor storeowner
Melvin Paes - police commissioner of Goi
Jo Tavares - forensics investigator

About the Author

Sheema Biswas is the author of The Upturning, with a Master's degree in English literature and an editorial background. A west coast native, the author now lives in New England with her family.